BARE TRAP

BARE TRAP

KEVIN ALDRICH

For Holly, Jayda, and Taegon

CONTENTS

1

WHILE BRIN WALLACE stomped through the silent forest, her boots sinking into the soft dirt with each step, she did her best to clear her mind. She took deep breaths of the wet, fecund air. She took pains to notice the beauty of the moss hanging on the Douglas Firs, the creaking of the trunks in the wind from the ocean, the ferns growing everywhere, their fronds vibrant green against the dark, moist tree trunks and the brown needles strewn on the ground. She tried to listen to the stillness in the air, the silence, the peace away from the cacophany of her normal life.

In other words, she did all the things her friends told her to do. Some days it helped. On other days, like today, it didn't.

Brin was not a natural hiker. Born and raised in downtown Chicago, far from the nearest forest, she'd come to the University of Portland for college and stuck around, as much from inertia as anything else. She'd partied a bit too much at UP and had been dumped into the workforce with few qualifications and fewer job prospects. She'd made ends meet by working as a barista in one of Portland's ubiquitous artisanal coffee shops.

She knew almost as little about coffee as she did about

hiking, but she'd at least drunk coffee before she took the job. But she learned fast, worked hard, and was easy on the eyes. Auburn hair, bright green eyes, and a flat stomach went a long way in the service industry.

Plus, she could bullshit as well as anyone. That's how she'd graduated on time, after all. She'd been hired on the spot at Kelly's Coffee in the Pearl and had worked her way up to lead barista over the last four aimless years.

She'd come home from work early a few months back when the power cut out on the whole block and shut Kelly's down for the day. Judging from the lack of clothing on her boyfriend and the slut in bed with him, he hadn't been expecting Brin home quite so early.

Brin had put up with a lot from Evan, mainly because he made her laugh and was good in bed, but no one cheated on Brin Wallace.

Ever.

Evan's shit had been on the curb before the slut had even found her panties.

Brin was perfectly happy without him. She didn't need some idiot man to make her feel whole. But, she had found herself with a lot of free time on her hands.

And a lot of pent up anger.

And it wasn't just from that cheating fuck Evan. Brin had had plans. She'd partied a lot, sure, but she'd always thought she'd go somewhere in life. And now here she was, halfway through her twenties, pulling espresso shots for Portland hipsters, sleeping with losers, and generally clocking time, going nowhere at all.

She wasn't interested in going to bars and listening to poetry slams or singer-songwriters on open mic nights with her friends. She didn't want to "get back out there" or "meet someone new". She wanted to get her life on track, and she needed to clear her head to do it.

That's why when her friends had suggested she take up hiking, Brin decided to give it a shot. Get close to nature. Find herself by wandering in the Oregon forests.

And, if nothing else, mix things up a bit.

Brin had hiked every day for the last two months, picking a different trail every time. She started easy with the Mount Tabor and Washington Park loops, then Hoyt Arboretum. Finding these a bit too tame, not challenging enough to clear her mind, she stepped up to the Marquam trail and Tryon Creek.

But these were still too easy. Brin was trim, muscular, and strong. She'd always been athletic and had made All-State as a center midfielder her junior and senior years. She could run a 5K without breaking a sweat.

She upped the difficulty another notch and hiked all thirty miles of the Wildwood Trail in one long day, getting up before dawn one weekend in late fall and coming home well after dark.

Still not enough.

She'd definitely gotten closer to nature than she'd ever been before. But, so far, she was no closer to getting her shit together.

This time, she'd decided to branch out beyond Portland and head to the coast. She wound up in Oswald West State Park in search of some real woods, something that might finally pop her out of her own head.

Brin pulled up the zipper on her red Patagonia shell to keep out the chill. The mists rolled in fast in Oregon, especially this close to the ocean. She'd opened her jacket just an hour earlier because she was sweating from the climb up to the summit of Neahkahnie Mountain. It wasn't a long hike, but it was an inter-esting and physical one, with all the switchbacks through the Sitka spruce and then, breaking out of the trees, the views along the trail all the way to the summit. Brin could see up and down the coast and out over the ocean, where the waves near shore sparkled in the sun, but a massive fog bank was moving in.

Brin had sat in the sunshine at the summit and watched the

fog roll in from over the ocean. It was surreal to see the mist roiling, like a time-lapse video in real-time, advancing inexorably toward her, filling the landscape and wisping in around her until her world of warmth and sunshine became gloomy, dark, and cold.

Brin had made her way back down the trail through the fog from the summit back into the spruce forest. She couldn't see more than a hundred feet in front of her and the trees which had been so green and welcoming earlier now leered, shadowy and sinister, high over her head.

She stuffed her hands into the pockets of her jacket and lengthened her stride. On the way up, she'd passed a few people headed in the other direction, but now she was alone on the trail. The thick fog made her feel like she was walking through a dark dreamscape.

She came to the trailhead and turned left down the gravel road toward Manzanita, where she'd left her car. The fog was still thick, but the wide, clean gravel road relaxed her. She hadn't realized how tense she'd become while walking through that creepy forest. The crunch of the gravel under her feet felt more like civilization. Like humans putting shit where it didn't naturally belong.

That felt more like home.

Where there had been a couple of cars parked earlier, there was no one now but Brin, the fog, and the crunching gravel. She knew that Highway 1 was somewhere up ahead, but at the moment she felt like she was in a grey bubble, out of time and space.

Brin wasn't entirely sure if she'd missed a turn somewhere, missed the trail back toward Manzanita where she'd left her car. She had no cell signal yet, and the low visibility and the absolute stillness of the air, suddenly without even a breeze, was disorienting for Brin. The thick stands of forest on either side of the trail must be blocking the breeze that carried the fog inland.

Brin lost track of direction in the featureless landscape. Nothing but the gravel underfoot, the crunching in her ears, and gray all around and above her. She tuned out the world, retreating into her thoughts under the hypnotic rhythm of her footsteps.

She heard voices in her head. Evan yelling at her, his clothes bunched up in his hands to cover his crotch, standing on the porch with his bare ass to the street after Brin had kicked him out. Her mother, ever supportive, ever cheerful, with just a hint of worry and disappointment growing more and more noticeable behind the cheer with every phone call.

Then she head other voices, ones she did not recognize. Men's voices.

Brin stopped walking.

Without the sound of the gravel, the silence smothered her. She closed her eyes and extended her hearing, willing the voices inside her head to quiet down.

She heard it again.

To her left. At least two voices, one deep, the other higher.

Maybe they were on the trail she was trying to find. Maybe they were on the road back to Manzanita.

Brin stepped gingerly forward, trying to make as little noise in the gravel as possible so she could keep track of the voices.

She lost them and stopped again.

After a long minute when she could only hear her heart beating, she picked up the voices once more. Faint. Further away, directly to her left.

Brin looked ahead at the gravel path, then to her left. Into the trees and the mist.

The gravel was the safer path, for sure. But had she already missed her turn? If so, where would she wind up if she kept on the gravel path?

Fuck it, thought Brin.

She turned left into the trees.

Brin moved quickly, but stepped lightly so that she could

listen for the men talking. Their voices came intermittently, faint at first, then louder as she gained speed and confidence, moving over the soft, mossy turf and through the trees.

Finally, the voices were loud enough that Brin didn't need to strain to hear them. The tightness that had crept back into her chest began to loosen once again.

There. In a clearing up ahead, maybe twenty yards through the trees. She saw a man's face in profile.

Dark beard on his face and short dark hair receding on his head. Tall. Older.

As Brin got closer, she saw that what she had thought was a beard was actually a tattoo that emerged from the collar of his black button-down shirt and ran up his neck.

He was looking down at something. Brin heard a different voice, another man's voice, high-pitched. Almost... frantic.

The man she could see didn't look like he was dressed for hiking. The road to Manzanita must be close by.

Brin heaved a sigh. Her shoulders relaxed.

She raised her hand, about to wave and call out, still ten yards and several trees away.

Then the man with the neck tattoo, the man with the short dark receding hair and the black button-down shirt raised his arm.

Blocked by a tree, Brin couldn't see what he held in his hand.

But she heard it.

A gunshot.

The high-pitched voice, the almost frantic voice, stopped.

Immediately.

So did Brin.

Along with her heart.

In that moment, her breath stopped. The voices in her head stopped. All thinking stopped.

She could hear the echo of the gunshot.

She could see the wisp of smoke from the muzzle rising in the air ahead of her.

She could hear the creak of a tree trunk as the breeze suddenly picked up again.

In that moment, time stood still.

Then, Brin ran.

2

James Pollard didn't like being called "Jim". Yet, no matter how many times he made that clear, people still insisted on calling him Jim. No amount of wealth or fame, such as it was, seemed to make a difference. It was still "Hey, Jim, good to see you" or "Jim, buddy, have I got a deal for you". All from people who didn't know James. All from people who just wanted something from James. All from people who didn't give a shit about James at all.

And that was all the people.

That was why James left.

Part of the reason, anyway, why he'd left all of them behind.

And those selfish vultures had moved on to the next cash cow, the next phenom with too much money and too few years to see those vultures for what they were, to know how to stand up for himself.

It was the way of life.

It was just like here in the forest where James now lived his life. Here, the Douglas squirrel ate nuts and seeds and the coyotes ate the Douglas squirrel. The black-tailed deer ate shrubs and trees and the mountain lion ate the black-tailed deer.

In Silicon Valley, the young tech entrepreneurs ate Soylent and organic artisanal arugula and the money vultures ate the young tech entrepreneurs.

The circle of life.

James had finally gotten rich enough quick enough that even the greediest Valley vultures couldn't feed fast enough to suck him dry before he made his escape. He'd fled north to the Oregon coast to build a utopian life. By definition, that meant a life without other people. Sarte was right after all.

He'd worked hard to learn to live off the land as much as possible. He'd used his surprising wealth–surprising, most of all, to James himself–to build a home that was sustainable and ecological. He'd built down into the ground to utilize geothermal heat and the natural insulation of the earth to moderate the temperature in his home, as well as to leave the profile of the land undisturbed; he had taken pains with the builders to reconstruct the landscape after building was complete to be as close as possible to the way James had first seen it when scouting for locations.

It wasn't perfect, of course. A four thousand square foot home had been implanted into the earth, after all, and there were vents and windows and doors that couldn't be avoided. Still, James was proud every time he approached his home to see how easy it was to miss it. How smoothly it blended into the natural landscape of the forest.

He thought that again as he approached the house. Especially now, when the mist had rolled in, if he hadn't known what to look for, James didn't think he'd be able to see the house at all. The front door was cleverly hidden behind a large boulder that was split down the center. The vents were covered in a material that resembled the local sphagnum moss perfectly. Only the windows gave away the home, and those were coated in a substance that eliminated reflections entirely in all but the brightest, most direct sunlight. In fog like this, they couldn't be seen at all unless you were standing in front of them and knew they were there.

And even then, you had to look hard to find them.

Yes, James was proud of his creation. It had taken years to find the spot, another year to find a discreet builder and get the permits in order, then an obscene amount of money to complete the build.

And that didn't even include the tech.

James wanted to live in the woods, utterly alone, but tech was in his blood. His utopia allowed him complete control over his home and the surrounding environment and allowed him to keep tabs on the world at large while still maintaining near total isolation.

The only exception was the occasional run down the mountain to collect those provisions he couldn't live without. Aluminum or hardwood for the CNC machine, carbon fiber or polycarbonate filaments for the 3D printers, Lactaid cottage cheese or white fudge-covered Oreo minis (James hadn't yet kicked the habit) and the like would be delivered to a series of lockboxes James had installed in a location that could be accessed by USPS, UPS, FedEx and his local grocery delivery service, but that couldn't be connected in any way to his home. It could be accessed easily from the front by road, for those who knew it was there, but could also be accessed from the back by a well-hidden trail that only James used. Wireless cameras hidden in the trees allowed James to be sure the area was clear before he went in to pick up his deliveries and haul them back to the house.

Those same cameras and a series of motion sensors were arrayed throughout the forest for a full concentric mile around James' home, allowing him total awareness of any hikers who may have wandered a bit too far off the beaten path.

Or intrepid reporters following whispers and rumors in search of a "Where is he now?" story.

Today, the run was for a delivery of rigid foam for some prototype side tables James was working on, a few bags of Lactated Ringer's solution for IV therapy, and more flour and yeast to replenish his stocks. James hauled it all up the hill from the lockboxes in a large camping backpack.

Keyed to James' biometrics, the front door unlocked and swung open when it detected his proximity to the exterior of the home. It only worked for him, of course. It swung open now and James entered and set the backpack down in the food storage room, unloading the flour and yeast into vacuum-sealed storage bins before bringing the foam downstairs to the machining lab.

James had banks of monitors arrayed throughout the house. Each bank contained four high-definition screens, the screens divided into a series of boxes. Each box displayed the view from one of his cameras. Between the cameras outside the house and those on the inside, there were sixty-four boxes arranged on the screens, sixteen per screen. A fifth screen showed the readings from the array of sensors around the property, from motion detectors to heat sensors to the current setting on the thermostat and the weather report for the next five days. James had these banks distributed so that he could always see one screen bank or another, no matter where in the home he was.

That was how the motion caught his eye when he had finished stowing the prototype foam in the materials closet. It was just a flash of red in the corner of his eye, but it was enough to draw his attention.

James walked closer to the bank of monitors, searching the boxes for that red flash.

He saw it again. James had the camera views arranged by physical layout, so the red shape moved from one box to the adjacent box, then to the one beside that.

The red flash turned out to be a person. A hiker.

No, a runner.

Someone was running through the forest.

It seemed to be a woman.

She was running fast. A bit wild.

Running toward the ridge.

One camera caught a glimpse of her face. James touched the screen to pause the feed in that box, then swiped to rewind until he could see a still image of the face.

The woman was young, younger than James. Her red hair streamed across her face, blown back by her running as she looked behind over her shoulder. Her eyes were captivating, a seafoam green color James had never seen in a human iris before. They were enhanced by the red in the strands of hair around them.

The eyes were wide with fear.

Whoever this was, she was running away from something. Something that had her running scared.

And running directly toward the boulder that concealed James' front door.

He scanned the other boxes to catch up to her current position. Hopefully, she would have changed course, turned right to move parallel to the ridge, not perpendicular.

She moved into frame. She hadn't changed course.

That boulder was twenty-two feet high at its peak.

She was headed right for it.

There was nothing James could do to stop it.

Though he had microphones arrayed with the cameras so he could hear what was happening outside, he had never bothered to install speakers. He could not imagine a circumstance where he would ever want to speak to someone or something outside. It would be too risky, too likely to reveal his position, his presence.

For a short moment, he regretted that choice now. He could have warned the woman.

She was approaching the ridge now, approaching the peak of the boulder.

Maybe she would see it.

Maybe she would realize and turn aside.

Maybe she would notice and jump at the last minute.

Or maybe not.

3

BRIN'S HEAD had never been so sore in her life. Not even after her first and last sorority party freshman year, when she'd learned what Jell-O shots and pot brownies were. And that they didn't mix.

But this soreness was worse.

It started in her head, like a white-hot fireplace poker stabbed through her temples to a spot right behind both eyes. From there, it radiated down her spine to her lower back, which was locked tight like a seized motor. It ended in her left leg, which somehow felt at once like it was on fire and like it was completely numb. Her skin itched and burned, but she couldn't feel her toes and couldn't move her leg at all.

She kept her eyes closed, but she heard a faint, regular beeping and a periodic clicking and whirring, accompanied by a pressure on her left arm. She could feel the softness of a bed beneath her body, a pillow beneath her head. She felt like she must be in a hospital, but there was none of the hospital stench of death and disinfectant that Brin despised. This place smelled like wood and... cloves.

She faded in and out of sleep, with her conscious episodes

getting longer and longer each time. She decided to brave opening her eyes.

Instant regret.

A bright white light directly above her head drove twin spikes into her eyes, spearing pain through to the very back of her skull. She wouldn't have been surprised if the pillow under her head now had two deep holes in it.

She cried out with surprise and pain.

"Sorry... stupid."

The voice was soft and low. It was followed by a click, then the light that Brin hadn't even realized was behind her eyelids went dark.

Brin tried again, fluttering her eyelids this time, testing the light.

It was darker in the room now, gentler. She was able to maintain a half squint for a while, using her eyelashes as filters until her eyes could adjust to being used again.

It took a minute before she could comfortably keep her eyes open. When she could, she saw only blurred shapes. A big brown shape that must have been the ceiling. Some bright, flashing fuzzy green shapes that must have been lights or some kind of monitor. A large white shape that filled her vision for a moment, then moved away.

"One twenty-four..." the soft, low voice muttered again, "seven... still high. Better..."

Brin's throat felt like a cat's scratching post. Her mouth was parched. It tasted like metal and vomit. She tried to speak, had to pry her lips apart like opening a Ziplock bag, but only a gasp of air came out. She tried to lick her lips to wet them, but her tongue felt like a giant tampon.

On second thought, Brin decided to just grunt for a while until her situation improved. Her first attempt was more like a long groan than a grunt, but it served its purpose.

"What is it?" said the voice. "What do you need?" It sounded more like the voice was talking to itself than to Brin.

The large white shape came back. It slowly resolved into a large rectangular shape with two long, thin rectangles on either side. This must be the source of the voice.

"Um... water?" it said.

Brin nodded. Her head felt like a wrecking ball was smashing into it with each nod.

After a minute, she felt a straw probe her lips and managed to part them enough to pull in the cool, clean water. Brin had never tasted water so good. It was like drinking liquid sunshine, like it was cleansing her soul as it rolled down her throat and into her stomach.

She took another pull, then another. Bliss overcame her. Brin let her head loll contentedly to one side and fell into sleep again.

The next time she woke, her left arm felt cold and her head was fuzzy. It still hurt, as did her leg and back, but it felt like someone else's pain, like she were visiting a good friend in the hospital after a car accident. When she opened her eyes, the bright light, mercifully, was still off, but the fuzzy shapes were even fuzzier than before. It seemed like there were two brown shapes and a dozen flashing green shapes.

She heard some kind of moaning noise that sounded far off, like a wounded animal was lying in the corner of the room. After a moment, Brin realized that moaning was coming from her.

"Pain medicine," said that voice again. The white shape was now blue in her vision. "Sorry to wake you. It'll kick innnnn soooooooooon."

Her vision took on a dark vignette that swirled into the center. Brin felt like she would hurl. Then everything went dark again.

When next she woke, she kept her eyes shut for a moment. Her head was still sore, but the pain wasn't blinding like it had been. Now, it was just a dull ache behind her eyes, and her head felt like it was full of bread dough. Her back was sore, too, but bearable.

The pain in her leg was a different story. It itched like mad, and every time Brin moved, it seared with pain like someone was holding her leg bones against a grinding dremel.

But her hearing was sharper. She could clearly hear a regular beeping noise that kept time with the heartbeat thumping in her chest. And she heard and felt the blood pressure cuff inflate periodically. Beyond that, she could make out sounds of movement in the background. Running water. A clang of metal, like bowls knocking. Footsteps, faint at first, then drawing closer. A sliding sound, almost pneumatic, that she couldn't place.

She heard the footsteps approach the bed, could feel someone standing beside her. There was a tapping noise.

Brin opened her eyes halfway, carefully letting her eyes adjust, testing the light, before opening them fully.

A man was leaning over her, fiddling with something above her head. She couldn't see his face, but his shirt was sky blue and loose. As he leaned, it fell against her shoulder. It smelled amazing, like sunshine and warm leather. Brin turned her head and closed her eyes to take a better sniff. She wanted to bunch it up under her nose and fall back asleep, inhaling that scent. She sighed with pleasure.

"Oh, sorry," said the man, pulling back, sadly bringing his shirt with him. "I didn't realize you were awake."

His voice was as soft as before, though Brin knew she was no longer addled by sleep or drugs. The guy just had a soft voice.

She opened her eyes again and found the face to go with the voice.

Tall. Lean and muscular. Nerdy, but in a healthy, athletic way. Thick dark straight hair, shaved on the sides and swept over from the top to hang over one ear like a wave curling. He had full lips and a two-day stubble.

Was she still hallucinating? Was this one of those hot doctor dreams?

He clicked on a penlight and leaned in, pulling the light from outside each ear and in toward her eyes. He was staring intently at her, looking deep into her eyes. Testing for something, Brin was sure.

But she didn't care. She was looking straight back at his eyes. Dark brown, but somehow clear and deep, too, with flecks of orange in their depths.

Jesus, Brin. Pull your shit together.

She closed her eyes and swallowed hard.

It hurt.

"Water," Brin rasped.

"Of course," said the man. He pulled a cup of water with a straw from a side table. It was cool and soothing, like before. Brin drained half the cup.

After drinking her fill, Brin took a look around. She was in a hospital bed with an IV in her right arm and a pulse oximeter on the index finger of her right hand. She had a blood pressure cuff on her left arm.

The floor was slate tile, nicer than any hospital she'd ever been in. The ceiling was higher than usual and had exposed wood beams running across. If this was a hospital, it was a damn fancy one.

Brin refocused on the man's face, still hovering over her.

She ignored the handsome features, the deep brown eyes.

Brin tried to sit up, but the pain in her leg flared, bringing tears to her eyes.

She squeezed her eyes shut and let herself fall back onto her pillow. She took a deep breath to collect herself.

She'd just seen someone murdered in cold blood. She wasn't going to let this asshole kidnap her.

No matter how hot he was.

Brin opened her eyes and fixed them on the man.

"Where am I," she asked, her voice like sandpaper, "and who the fuck are you?"

4

THE GREEN of the woman's eyes was even brighter than it had been on the video screen. They'd been closed all this time, so James hadn't been able to see them before. But now, they were open and liquid with tears. The light from the room refracted in the tears and enhanced the natural color of her irises, green like the patina of weathered copper. A startling, honest green.

The effect made James' heart jump in his chest, hitched his breath.

It distracted him so much, he didn't hear what the woman had said.

"I'm sorry?" James stammered.

"I said," the woman replied, snapping each word, "where am I and who the fuck are you?"

"Oh, um..."

James couldn't tell her where they were. The woman's leg was broken, but it would be well enough in a few days for her to make the trip down the mountain. James didn't want to compromise his location.

Of course, bringing her down the mountain would do just that. James just hadn't hadn't had time yet to figure out how to get the woman to safety without giving her any clues to her location. For the time being, he would just resort to vagaries.

"You're in my home."

The woman's eyes narrowed with suspicion. She peeked under the bedsheet. Her eyes widened for a moment, then fulled with fury.

"No, you…" James stammered again, "not like that or anything. You fell." James gestured vaguely toward the upstairs, toward the front door. "You fell off a ridge and landed in front of my door. I only removed your clothing so I could assess your injuries."

Now the woman's brows furrowed, too. She wasn't buying any of this.

"It's true," James said, holding up his hands, palms out. "You can watch the footage from the security cameras."

This seemed to stop the woman for a moment.

"Wait," she said, "you have it all on video?"

"Yes," said James. He gestured behind him to one of the video screens. "Yes, I have a lot of security cameras. They record when any sound or movement is detected. I store all of the recordings."

The girl tried to sit up again. James wasn't sure it was a great idea, but she seemed determined, so he found the remote, showed her how to raise the back of the bed to a more upright position, and left the remote in her lap.

After the exertion, the woman closed her eyes and furrowed her brow again. She looked like she was in pain. Probably still had a headache from the concussion, exacerbated by the sudden shift in position.

"You said I fell," said the woman.

"Yes," replied James. "You fell of the ridge above my house, landed pretty hard. You sustained a concussion with emesis, some bruising and swelling on your spine from L3 to L5."

James stood and grabbed a tablet off the table at the end of the bed. He tapped a few buttons and called up the woman's X-rays, turned the tablet to show her, swiping through the ventral image, then the lateral.

"No apparent loss of sensation from the swelling, though. You were still responding to stimuli. Can you wiggle your toes?"

The bed sheet moved above the woman's feet. She winced in pain, but the movement was there. A little early to be sure, maybe, but James didn't think there would be any serious problems from the lumbar contusions.

He swiped on the tablet again.

"Oh," James said, gesturing to the X-ray that came up, "there is a tibia fracture, too."

"My leg is broken?" said the woman, her eyes shooting wide.

"It's okay, it's okay," said James. He pointed to the X-ray, bringing the tablet closer.

The woman took it from him.

"See," said James, "it's an oblique fracture. Complete, but stable. That was from before. If you go to the next one…"

The woman swiped to the next image.

"See?" said James. "That's after I set the leg and applied the cast. I barely had to reduce it at all. Just put the cast on. Good to go. Pretty lucky, really."

The woman lifted the bedsheet again, higher, and peered down at her leg. She let it fall back down and swiped again through the X-rays on the tablet.

"Are you a doctor?" she asked.

A reasonable question.

"Well, no," said James. "But I have some… training. And I'm well equipped here to deal with most common medical situations."

"Why didn't you bring me to a hospital?"

Another reasonable question.

"You were unconscious," said James. "And you had vomited. I have equipment here, so the safest thing to do was to assess your condition here. I saw that your break was fairly straightforward, but I didn't think I could get you down the mountain without worsening your condition."

Truth was, James didn't have a good way to get her down safely, and he was pretty sure he wouldn't be able to carry her unconscious with a broken leg. Odds are, if he had tried he would have slipped or tripped and they'd both have ended up in the hospital. Assuming they were found, which wasn't a guarantee at all.

The woman dropped her head back against the pillow, shutting her eyes and shading them with one hand, rubbing her temples. With the other hand, she held the tablet out for James to take.

"Are you in pain again?" asked James. "I won't ask you to rate it on a scale of smiley faces," he smiled, "but I can give you more pain meds, if you need them."

"Why not just drive me to the hospital?" she said.

Ignored the offer of pain meds. Good sign.

"Like I said, I have the equipment here and it was safer..."

"Take me there now, then," said the woman. She threw off the bed covers. She was wearing a typical hospital gown. James had several folded in the supply room. If you're going to build something, you might as well build it right. All the way down to the hospital gowns.

The woman swung her good leg over the side of the bed and reached down with both hands to swing over her other leg, too. She closed here eyes and started to wobble. James moved forward just as the woman pitched forward. She would have landed face-first on the tile floor, but James was able to stop her and help her back to a reclining position on the bed.

He held his hands on her shoulders, gently pushing her back

against the bed. She just looked up at him with those startling green eyes.

"I don't think you should go anywhere just now," said James, his voice a hoarse whisper.

5

AT FIRST, Brin had just been confused. Confused and in pain.

Then, when she saw that she was dressed in nothing but a hospital gown, she'd been sure for a second that this guy was some kind of hot psycho who had drugged her and raped her and was keeping her locked up in this weird hospital basement.

But as soon as that thought came, she knew it wasn't true. She would know if she'd been raped.

But that just made the situation even weirder. Who the fuck has a hospital bed in their house? This guy had the monitors and the IV drip and everything. It was like she'd stumbled into a movie set or something.

Then he mentioned the security footage. Brin was back to the psycho hypothesis again, only without the sex-crazed misogyny. This was just some kind of paranoid weirdo.

Then he pulled out the X-rays.

That was too weird to even be true. Weird enough that Brin couldn't even process the fact that the guy was even able to take X-rays.

In his house.

In the woods.

She just focused on the X-rays themselves.

Brin was no radiologist, but she agreed with him. It was obvious from the image of her leg that it was broken, but that the break was clean.

She hoped to God this psycho weirdo at least knew what he was doing with the medical stuff. Brin really didn't want to be gimping around for the rest of her life because this guy wanted to play doctor.

Despite the circumstances, though, Brin's gut was telling her this guy wasn't really a psycho. Weird, for sure, but not dangerous. She really believed that he was trying to help her.

She just wasn't sure if he knew what he was doing.

Nonetheless, she didn't have a whole lot of choice at this point. She couldn't even stand up. She'd almost passed out when she'd tried.

And the guy wouldn't drive her to the hospital.

"Why not call 9-1-1?" Brin asked.

The guy shook his head. A piece of hair fell down over one of his eyes. Absentmindedly, he swept it back.

Brin's heart fluttered.

"The nearest access road is a twenty minute hike from here. They'd need to bring a stretcher up through the woods and it's pretty rocky." He gestured toward Brin. "As you discovered."

She remembered running through the forest, though she couldn't recall why. She remembered running and she remembered the ground falling away beneath her, the sky tilting all crazy.

That must have been the fall.

Brin was glad she couldn't remember the impact.

"Plus," continued the man, "it's almost nighttime. Getting up the hill is hard enough when it's light out. It'd be too difficult in the dark."

Brin had other questions. How did the guy get back and forth from work? How did he get food and supplies? Where did he park his car?

But, her concentration was flagging. She was starting to feel sleepy again, the pain in her leg still burning and her headache pounding like an angry toddler against her skull.

Brin leaned back against the bed and closed her eyes. She had ignored the man's offer of pain medication earlier. She was in a strange place with a very strange man and she wanted to stay clear-headed. With the pain in her head, she was starting to regret that choice.

"Are you okay?" asked the man. "Do you need pain meds."

She did. She wanted to fall into that deep black hole and sleep until the pain went away.

But, she couldn't.

She shook her head. The wrecking ball was back.

"If you're in pain, you should take something for it," said the guy, gently.

He really did seem like he was trying to help. He seemed like a nice guy.

But, so had Ted Bundy.

"Ibuprofen," mumbled Brin. Take the edge off without dulling her mind completely.

"Contraindicated with a concussion," the guy said. "How about acetaminophen?"

Brin furrowed her brow, trying to remember which one was acetaminophen.

"That's Tylenol," said the guy.

Right. Tylenol.

Brin nodded. The guy went off to fetch the meds.

Brin willed her eyes to open again while he was gone. She looked around the room, taking stock of her surroundings.

Tile floors. No windows. Room to her left, where the guy had gone for the meds. Door to her right, through which she could see a hallway and a staircase leading up. TV with a shitload of cameras views coming through.

She was hooked to an IV, but had no other restraints. Cast on one leg, blinding headache, wearing only a hospital gown. If she made a break for it, even if she got away she'd freeze outside without some clothes. And getting away would be a long shot with a bad leg and all of those cameras.

Brin pursed her lips. Looked like she might be stuck there for a while.

With the hot weirdo.

The hot weirdo brought the Tylenol and a cup of water. Brin downed them both.

"What's your name?" she asked.

"James," he replied. "Pollard. James Pollard."

He said it awkwardly. He said his own name awkwardly. It was kind of cute.

Weird, but cute.

"What's your name?" he asked.

Brin laughed.

"You took off all my clothes," she said. "Didn't you go through my stuff, too?"

James got a look on his face like that was the most horrific thing he'd ever heard.

"No, of course not," he said. "I would never invade your privacy that way."

"And stripping me naked isn't an invasion of privacy?"

He blushed bright red. "That was for medical reasons," he spluttered.

Brin had just been teasing the guy. She would absolutely have gone through his stuff, looking for some ID, someone to call, maybe a cell phone or something. But this guy was really offended by the idea.

"Okay, okay," said Brin. "Don't pop a gasket. I was just joking."

James settled down a bit, but still had a hurt look on his face.

This guy was unlike anyone Brin had ever met.

"I'm Brin," she said. "Brin Wallace."

James nodded.

"Good to meet you, then, Brin" he said.

"You too."

After an awkward pause, James turned to leave.

"And James?" said Brin.

James turned back.

"Thank you," Brin continued. "For helping me."

The hurt look finally faded from James' face. He nodded, than walked out the door and up the stairs.

Brin closed her eyes again.

First some sleep.

Then, figure out how to get the fuck out of here.

6

JAMES PORED over the surveillance videos, looking for clues. Who was Brin Wallace, and why was she running through the forest?

She'd been looking back over her shoulder as she ran. Who or what was she running from?

James used a facial recognition script to scan through all the day's footage on every camera to find Brin's earliest appearance. She'd come in from the north and had already been running scared when the first camera picked her up. James ran through the captures from that camera that were taken after Brin had passed, looking for a pursuer, human or animal.

He saw nothing.

Just the fallen leaves blown by the wind, and a couple of deer wandering by, munching on twigs.

The cameras were activated by motion and sound. James had tweaked their sensitivity to hair-trigger levels. He had plenty of data storage, so there was no reason to skimp on the video recordings. There were around thirty video captures made from that camera in the few hours after Brin had passed through.

But no sign of anyone or anything pursuing her.

James went back downstairs to the sickbay—as a long-time Trekkie, that's how he thought of it—to check on Brin. She was still sleeping, her vitals normal and stable.

The broken leg was inconvenient, but straightforward. James hadn't made a leg cast before, but he had good materials and he'd found instructions online that were clear enough. YouTube was an incredible resource, really, one that was too often over-looked and dismissed in the sea of media stars and cat videos. And casting a leg wasn't rocket science. You didn't need a medical degree to wrap a person's leg in casting tape and fiberglass.

Setting the leg, on the other hand, could have been compli-cated. James had been a bit nervous before seeing the X-ray. Thankfully, the break had been clean, the reduction trivial.

It was the concussion that worried James. Brin had vomited, which was worrisome, but she'd only vomited once. That was a good sign. But, concussions were notoriously tricky. The CT scan showed no swelling or bleeding in her brain, but James wasn't a radiologist. The internet could only get you so far. He could have missed something, something small, in the images.

And small things had a tendency to become big things if they weren't given enough attention early on.

On top of that, the concussion made pain management tricky. James had plenty of pain medications, but he'd debated for a good hour whether or not to use them. He'd finally settled on a low dose of morphine just to take the edge off when he had first gotten Brin settled. He knew that it was important to regu-late pain to allow the body the peace it needed to heal itself. But, he didn't want to cause a brain bleed or induce any swelling.

Still, Brin had made it this far. With each passing hour, the risk from the concussion grew smaller and smaller. If something bad was going to happen as a result of the head injury, it would happen sooner rather than later.

James changed a few settings on the laptop next to Brin's bed to route her readings to his tablet so he could keep an eye on them without having to be next to the bed. Brin needed rest, and James didn't want to be tiptoeing around the room running the risk of waking her.

He pulled up the video feed from the sickbay on his tablet, as well, took it back upstairs, pulled a double shot from the espresso machine in his kitchen, and sat in an armchair in his library.

If Brin made it through the night without incident, she'd be in the clear. James was going to keep an eye on her until he knew she would be okay.

He really didn't want to have to explain to the police how a dead woman ended up in his basement.

IT WASN'T PAIN that woke Brin. Nor was it a sound. The medical room was dark and quiet, the only sound the occasional beeping of her monitors or the buzzing of the blood pressure cuff as it inflated on her arm. What woke Brin was something much more mundane.

She had to pee.

Bad.

The hot weirdo James was nowhere in sight, and Brin wasn't about to shout his name until he came running. The damsel-in-distress routine really wasn't her style.

She sat up slowly and managed to swing her legs over the side of the bed without passing out. The tube connected to the needle in her arm draped over her shoulder. Brin traced it back to a saline bag hanging from a hook behind the bed. Fortunately, the hook was attached to a pole with wheels.

An instant crutch.

Brin swung the pole around the bed and used it to wedge herself up to a standing position, leaning all of her weight on her good leg. Even with the cast, she wasn't sure how much weight her bad leg would hold.

Plus, she didn't know how good a job James had really done

when he set it and put the cast on. And she didn't want to find out by faceplanting into the tile floor.

She peered through the dark room, lit only by the light from the monitor, a ceiling light dimmed low, and floor lights arrayed at intervals around the room and in the hallway. She didn't see a bathroom, so she headed toward the adjoining room, where James had gone to get her medicine. There had to be a bathroom in there.

The room wasn't a room at all, but a hub, with a series of five rooms radiating out from the central room in which she stood. Every room had large windows in the wall so that Brin could see all the way in from the hub. One room held what looked like an X-ray machine. Another some kind of MRI or CAT scan machine.

A third room was an operating theater, though what kind of weird shit not-a-doctor James thought he'd get up to in there, Brin didn't even want to know.

The fourth room was narrower. It just held a bunch of computers, black boxes blinking away in racks from floor to ceiling.

The fifth room was a supply room, with cabinets and shelves covering every wall. Brin saw needles in plastic packages, tape and wraps and gauze of all kinds, bedding and gowns and masks and gloves. In the glass-fronted cabinets, she saw rows and rows of bottles and boxes filled with medicine. There seemed to be a full pharmacy in there.

This guy was a grade-A nut job.

Or he just had delusions of grandeur and had watched too much Doogie Howser as a kid.

Brin didn't really have time to dwell on it, though, because she was about to piss on the floor right there and then.

In the supply room, she spotted a pair of crutches. She grabbed them and hobbled back into the other room, past her bed, and into the hallway, the crutches in one hand and the IV pole in the other.

The hallway was wide and elegant, with the same slate tile floors as the room with her hospital bed. It was elegant, but short, with only the stairs leading up and a door beside it.

Brin tried the door, hoping for a bathroom.

The door was locked.

Brin sighed, looking down at her hand, where her IV needle was taped down.

Huh. The thought hadn't occurred to her before now, but the weirdo had stuck her vein while she'd been unconscious and set up a working IV. That took some skill. Maybe his delusions weren't quite as bad as she thought.

Still a weirdo, though.

And Brin hated needles.

Regardless, she had to pee and she couldn't climb the stairs with the IV pole. She carefully peeled back the tape over the needle. Gritting her teeth and squeezing her eyes shut, she gently slid the needle out of her hand. Blood welled up around the site of the needle stick, but she wasn't about to go back for a band-aid.

With her crutches in one hand and her other hand on the stair railing as support, Brin hopped up the stairs on her good leg. Just like she used to do when training for soccer. One-leg stair hopping was great for building calf and thigh strength.

Not so great when your bladder was about to burst.

Thankfully, there was a bathroom just at the top of the stairs.

Once she had relieved herself and rinsed off her hand in the sink, using a wad of toilet paper to staunch the bleeding, Brin decided to explore the house a little.

The hallways on this floor were also wide, with the same slate tile on the floors. Must have cost a fortune, but it was very helpful as Brin went swinging through the house on her crutches.

The first room she passed was another storage room. Long and thin, the room was lined with metal shelves from floor to ceiling. The shelves held plastic bins that were filled with electronics parts and gear. There were wires rolled into neat coils, circuit boards, disembodied keyboards and monitor screens. A stack of laptops sat on one shelf, a neat row of flat-screen TVs on another, a bin of fans in small, square enclosures on a third.

Brin wasn't sure if she was still in the weirdo's house or if she'd somehow stumbled into the last Radio Shack on the planet.

The next room she came to was even stranger. It was a large room with two massive boxes inside that were big enough almost for Brin to step into. Each one had some kind of computer screen attached to the front, with a glass door that enclosed some kind of metal arm inside the box.

One of the boxes was whirring softly. Brin didn't want to turn on the light, didn't want to let James know she was sneaking around. But, there was enough glow from the indicator lights on the box itself to see something inside the box that looked like a leg with sticks attached at the top. A metal arm was moving around the leg with some kind of dremel, shaving material away, hollowing out the inside of the leg. Some kind of vacuum system would suck out the shavings as they fell on the floor of the box.

Brin wasn't sure what the box was. Some kind of manufacturing machine, it seemed. But she didn't know what James was making. She glanced down at the cast on her leg. Did he make that cast in one of these machines? The cast looked like the cast she'd had on her wrist in high school, and like every other cast she'd ever seen.

She moved on. Beside those large boxes was a shelf of smaller boxes, ranging from the size of a mini-fridge to the size of a toaster oven. Each one had a similar glass door on the front and a metal arm or metal rails on the inside.

Beside those, on another shelf, were several contraptions

that looked like old typewriters with the housing taken off. Typewriters or weaving looms.

They were all various kinds of machine, but Brin had never seen machines like that before.

The room had two doors and no windows. She continued on through the second door and came to a wide room with a massive computer monitor on a desk in one corner. Against two walls were tables strewn with large, curling papers.

A lamp behind the monitor on the computer desk cast a dim glow across the room. Brin could see that the papers were blueprints or diagrams of some kind. There were crude sketches of legs bent at the knee, climbing stairs and running. They had arrows and mathematical formulas all over them. It reminded Brin of the problems she'd been forced to solve in Physics class in high school.

Maybe James was building a robot.

Seemed like something he would do.

Brin continued through that room, her crutches clicking against the tile floor with each swinging step. The next room was a huge library, with books in shelves built into the walls from floor to ceiling. A floor lamp was lit in the corner. Brin could see a ladder on a black metal rail leaning against one wall. A leather couch and several armchairs were distributed throughout the room, along with a coffee table and two side tables, both stacked with books.

As she moved through the room, Brin noticed with a start that one of the armchairs on the far side, hidden partly in shadow, was occupied.

James was sitting there.

"Oh," said Brin, "I didn't know you were there."

James didn't reply.

"What time is it, anyway?" Brin asked.

Still no reply.

She knew he was weird, but she hadn't pegged him as an

asshole. Most of the assholes Brin knew would have let her die on their doorstep. At best, they might have gone out for coffee and called 911 to clean up the mess. They certainly wouldn't have brought her inside and given her a full medical workup.

Brin moved closer, crutches creaking, and peered into the shadows. James sat there, a tablet glowing in his hand, but tilted at an odd angle across his lap.

He was asleep.

Brin smirked. Guess Doogie wore himself out.

Well, Brin couldn't deny that he'd earned the rest. And she was grateful for it.

She carefully worked her way behind the armchair. Using it for support, she reached over and switched off the light. The glow from the tablet in James' lap seemed twice as bright then. Brin glanced down and saw a readout of vital stats, all of which were flatlined and flashing red, since she was no longer attached to the sensors. Beside that readout was a camera view of her empty bed.

He'd been watching her.

Brin wasn't sure if that was creepy or sweet, if she should thank him or find something hard to knock him out with and run for the hills. Instead, she just moved on out of the room, clicking as softly as she could with the crutches against the tile floor, and left James to sleep.

The next room was a small kitchen, with a sink, a dishwasher, a pantry, and a refrigerator. In the center of the room was a small round table. On the counter was an espresso machine, a La Marzocco. Made in Florence, Italy. Expensive, and totally worth it. It looked like it had been used quite a bit recently. There were coffee grounds all over the catch basin, and the knock box was full of used pucks.

Brin moved on to the refrigerator and opened it up. The blue light from inside fell upon her like the glow from heaven. She could even hear the chorus of angels in her ears.

She hadn't realized how hungry she was until she saw the fridge stocked with water and iced tea, cheese, sliced turkey and ham, and produce of all kinds, from mushrooms and tomatoes to romaine lettuce and broccoli.

Brin grabbed some cheese, turkey, tomato, and romaine and dumped them on the counter. She found a pantry around the corner and discovered dijon mustard and thick-sliced bread that looked like it was homemade. She loaded up.

She was gonna make one hell of a sandwich.

She stacked the turkey and cheese high, cut the tomato thick, with salt and pepper, slathered the mustard on the bread, added the romaine for the crunch, then sat down at the table to dig in. Her stomach growled in anticipation even as she opened her mouth for the first bite. The crunch as she bit down was a sound of pure bliss.

"Please," said James from the doorway.

Brin, surprised, sucked in air at the sound, bringing half her food with it.

"Make yourself at home," James said.

8

Jᴀᴍᴇs sᴛᴏᴏᴅ in the doorway and watched Brin cough until her eyes watered. He was still groggy from waking up, but the truth was, he was angry with her.

And with himself.

"You shouldn't be up here," James said. "You should be resting."

Brin tried to reply, but could only cough every time she tried to draw air.

James walked to the fridge and pulled a bottle of water from it, twisted off the cap, and handed it to Brin. He sat down while she drank greedily, finally gasping great gulps of air.

"I had to pee," she said, once she'd finally recovered.

Shit. James had forgotten about that.

"Right," he said. "Sorry about that. I thought about a catheter during your initial exam, but..."

Brin's green eyes popped wide open.

"Well," continued James, "it didn't seem... appropriate."

There was only so far James would go with an unconscious patient, even for medical reasons.

"Jesus," said Brin, shaking her head. "I'm glad we agree on that."

"Yeah, well, I guess I forgot about your bladder in all of the excitement."

"You're forgiven," said Brin. "And, just for the record, my bladder is really none of your business, anyway."

They stared at each other for a beat.

He didn't really know if she was trying to be funny or not. Her bladder really was none of his business, but neither was any of the other stuff he'd already seen and done. Was she being ironic or just obvious? Was he just groggy from his nap?

James grinned.

"Understood," he said.

He looked at the clock on the wall. It was nearly sunup. He had only been asleep for about half an hour. Just couldn't keep his eyes open at the end, no matter how many shots of espresso he drank.

"In the morning, I want you to take me out of here," said Brin through a mouthful of sandwich. Bits of bread fell on the table as she spoke.

James sighed. "In the morning, I'll take you outside and you'll understand why that's impossible."

She wasn't going to just wait patiently for him to decide how to get rid of her. James was going to have to come up with a plan for getting her down the mountain without showing her exactly where he was.

Although, she could probably just backtrack from wherever she'd been when she started running. If she remembered what direction she'd gone, she'd be able to find his home again.

"How much do you remember from before your fall?"

Brin took another massive bite. Either she's starving or she eats like a frat boy. She thought while she chewed, staring into space, then shrugged.

"I just remember running through the woods," she said. "Then everything turned upside down and I woke up here."

Retrograde amnesia was not uncommon with concussions.

She'd likely get her memory back within the next day or two, though it could take longer.

But, if James could get rid of her before she did, there was a chance she wouldn't be able to piece enough together to reconstruct his location.

Still, he wouldn't compromise her health. It wasn't worth it just to keep one person from knowing where he lived. It was bound to get out one way or another. James was surprised and grateful that he'd gone as long as he had without being discovered. He'd lived in peace and solitude for nearly ten years.

Plus, Brin hadn't shown even a flicker of recognition when he'd told her his name. Maybe the world had just moved on and no one cared anymore what had become of James Pollard. He was no Steve Jobs or Mark Zuckerberg, anyway. He was never a household name. Just a celebrity among tech nerds and money chasers.

James relaxed just a bit. Maybe he was overreacting.

"Listen," he said as Brin polished off the last bite of the sandwich, reached back into the fridge for more water, and turned the bottle upside down into her mouth. "Once you're finished, I'll help you back to bed. You really shouldn't be walking around just yet."

Brin drained the water without taking it off of her lips. Definitely a frat boy.

"I'm fine," she said, wiping her mouth with the back of her hand. "I'm good with these crutches. Doesn't even hurt."

"Maybe so," James said, "but you should still get some more rest. You need to give your body time for the inflammation to reduce and healing to begin."

"I want to see those recordings," Brin said. "The ones from your surveillance cameras."

James chewed his lip. "I looked through those. I couldn't see anything suspicious on there after you came through. There was no one following you."

Brin didn't say anything, just played with the lid to the water bottle, spinning it noisily on the table.

She seemed like she was hiding something. But what could it be?

No, James was being paranoid. He was tired. And she probably was, too.

"Look, we both need rest, okay?" he said.

Brin nodded, reluctantly.

He helped her back downstairs, got the monitors and the IV —over Brin's protests—hooked back up, then climbed back up the stairs to his own bed.

Cleaning the kitchen could wait. James needed sleep.

9

THE MAN STARED down at Brin. She was on the ground, couldn't move.

On his neck, something wriggled and writhed, like it was inside his neck, just under his skin.

Something dark.

A snake.

No. A dragon.

The man held out his arm. Pointed at Brin.

The dragon squirmed again, then burst from the man's neck. It reared back, focused on Brin. Under the man's control.

It grew larger, larger, until its maw was big enough to swallow Brin whole.

She stared down the darkness of its throat. That darkness began to glow.

Brighter. Brighter.

As bright and fiery as the sun.

Brin tried again to move, to crawl away, to get up and run. Her limbs wouldn't respond.

She opened her mouth to scream.

But only the sound of a gunshot emerged.

44

"Hey. Brin."

Brin was shaking.

"Brin, wake up."

She was being shaken.

Brin bolted upright.

She was in the bed. Her chest was heaving with ragged breaths. She could feel her pulse in her temples and in her chest.

James was standing beside her.

Brin wiped her forehead with her hand. It came back slick with sweat.

She closed her eyes and breathed deep through her nose a few times, focusing on slowing her breath, slowing her heart rate.

Once she was under control, she opened her eyes again.

"What are you doing here?" she asked James.

He was barefoot, wearing workout shorts and a worn t-shirt a size too big for him. Dark circles ringed his eyes like a Halloween skeleton and his hair was mussed and wild, matted on one side and spiked on the other.

He looked like shit.

"You were having a nightmare," James said. "Your vitals were spiking. The alarms on my tablet woke me up."

"It was just a dream," said Brin.

"It was a bad one, then," replied James. "When I got down here, you were tossing your head back and forth and you had your hands up in the air."

"My hands... what?"

Brin struggled to remember the dream, but it was already fading. Something about a dragon. A black dragon.

"You were mumbling something, too," said James.

"What was I mumbling?"

"It sounded like 'no fire' or 'more fire', but I couldn't really make it out."

Jesus. He made her sound like a wack job.

Still, there was something about it. She couldn't remember the dream, but a feeling had settled in her chest, left there once the pounding of her heart had slowed. It was a tightness, like a fist of coal buried there.

Something was wrong. Something about that dream. Something Brin needed to remember.

And fast.

"You look like shit," she said to James.

"Yeah, well, I was fast asleep three minutes ago, so fuck you."

That might have been the first time Brin had heard James swear. It was certainly the first time he'd sworn at her.

She grinned.

Maybe he wasn't such a dweeb after all.

"Well, go back to sleep, then," said Brin. "You definitely need more beauty rest."

James grumbled something Brin couldn't hear as he turned and climbed back up the stairs.

For Brin, sleep was slow to return. She lay in the dark, listening to the sounds of her monitors, the beeping and the whirring, watching the green and red lights glow and flash in the darkness.

When she closed her eyes, she saw a different red glow. One that made her eyes fly open again every time.

She focused on her breathing.

Slow.

Slow.

Sleep, Brin.

Breathe slow.

Sleep.

And remember.

10

WHEN HE WOKE in the morning and went to the kitchen for a cup of coffee, Brin was already there. She was standing at the stove, scrambling eggs. They were sizzling in the frying pan. James could smell toast in the toaster. He moved to the espresso machine.

"Don't you fucking dare touch that espresso machine," said Brin without looking up from the eggs. "I saw last night in the knock box that pile of wet slop you called coffee. I won't allow you to desecrate a La Marzocco like that." She looked over her shoulder and speared James with a hard stare. "Not on my watch."

James sighed and sat down at the table.

"And thanks for the clothes," Brin said. "Felt kinda weird walking around in a hospital robe."

Last night, before falling back asleep, James had found a pair of wide-legged sweatpants, a t-shirt, and an old sweater. He'd left it on a chair in Brin's room before trudging upstairs to go back to sleep.

"I see you've heeded my medical advice yet again," James said. "I thought you were going to get some rest and stay off that leg."

"Yeah, well, you're not actually a doctor, so you can't actually give medical advice."

James rubbed his face. He'd slept much longer than usual, but he was still exhausted. He didn't have the energy to fight with Brin. If she wanted to fuck up her leg, that was her business.

"When am I going to get this magical coffee?"

"Oh, you're one of those customers?" said Brin. "I saw a hundred of you fuckers every day at work. Always think your drama is more important than everyone else's drama."

"It's more important to me."

Brin just snorted in response.

"Besides," continued James, "I don't go to coffee shops. That's why I bought these La Marzoccos. So I could have good espresso at home." He cleared his throat pointedly. "When I want it."

"I'm cooking your fucking breakfast, trying to say 'thank you'," said Brin. She dished the eggs onto a plate, put two pieces of toast beside them, and slid the plate in front of James. "So don't be such an asshole."

James looked down at the eggs. Scrambled with mushrooms and tomatoes, cheese melted throughout. Steam rising off of the plate. His stomach growled at the sight.

"Thank you," he said. He scooped a forkful onto a piece of toast and took a bite. The eggs were just the right amount of salty and peppery and came alive in his mouth, the hot cheese silky on his tongue.

He moaned involuntarily.

"Thank you very much," he said around his mouthful of food.

Brin arched an eyebrow at him as she set her own plate down, then turned to the espresso machine.

"What do you drink?" she asked. "Let me guess. Mocha decaf latte with rainbow sprinkles?"

"Double macchiato," James said.

Brin turned and nodded at him. "Well, well," she said. "Maybe there's hope for you yet."

James was halfway through his eggs when Brin slid the coffee in front of him. He eagerly brought it to his lips. Even before he took a sip, the smell of the coffee overwhelmed him. It was rich and sensuous. He'd never smelled coffee so good. Certainly not when he made it himself.

When he took a sip, he fell back in his chair. The taste was exquisite. Strong, but not bitter. Smooth and full, like the coffee were imparting its life story, and it had been a long and interesting life.

It brought James back to the trip he'd made to Italy when he first made a bit of money in Silicon Valley. That had been the first time he'd ever had coffee. When he got back to the States, nothing he tasted came close. From that moment on, he'd only used imported Italian coffee ground in imported Italian grinders and prepared in imported Italian espresso machines.

What he made was better than the shit he'd found at Starbucks, but still never came close to what he'd had in Italy.

Until now.

"Oh, thank you, thank you, thank you," he muttered, draining the rest of the tiny cup.

Brin had already pulled a second one for him. She just laughed and switched out the cups.

"Go easy on that one, James," she said. "I really don't want to see you wired. I don't think I could handle full nerd until I'm back to one hundred percent."

"Where'd you learn to make coffee like this?" asked James, forcing himself to eat more eggs before sipping from the second cup of coffee.

"Are you kidding?" replied Brin. "I'm head barista in a Portland coffee shop. If I didn't know my shit after my first two months, I would have been booted straight to the curb and bludgeoned with artisanal pencils by the customers."

James nearly inhaled a mouthful of eggs, but managed to swallow before he laughed out loud.

Brin smiled at him as she sat down with her own coffee and tucked in to her own plate of eggs.

James felt a warmth cover him from head to toe when he saw Brin's smile. A smile directed at him.

James shook his head. Maybe it was just the effect of the coffee, the caffeine washing over him, waking him up.

"You were going to show me around today," said Brin.

"I was?"

"Yes, you were. You said you would take me outside and show me why you couldn't take me to a real doctor until I was better."

"Right," nodded James. "I did say that, didn't I?"

There was no harm in that. Probably. The house was tucked into the side of a steep hill, with a tall ridge on top that was pretty inaccessible, especially for someone with a broken leg. The rest was just fairly dense forest. No landmarks or distinguishing characteristics, really, aside from the house itself.

Just as James had designed it.

In fact, after he'd first moved in, he'd gotten lost more than once trying to make his way back from a pickup.

"Yeah, okay," he said. "I'll take you outside." He finished the last bite of eggs and swallowed a sip of coffee.

"And I want to see the surveillance videos," Brin said.

"I told you I didn't see anything in them."

"I don't care. I still want to see them."

Brin looked James in the eye. His breath caught for a moment as the force of those clear green eyes took him by surprise.

"Please," she added.

James shrugged. "If you want to," he mumbled, and took a bite of toast to cover his discomfort.

"And then," Brin continued, "how about a tour of the house?"

James' discomfort disappeared in a wave of annoyance. Not only wouldn't she stay in bed like she needed to, she wasn't going to let James get anything done, either.

"Anything else, your highness?" he said.

Brin knocked back her own espresso in one gulp, then grinned at James.

"I'll let you know," she said.

James was going to have to figure out how to get Brin back to the real world and out of his hair.

Fast.

11

BRIN HAD WATCHED the video recordings first, while James showered and dressed. Like James, she hadn't seen any evidence of anyone pursuing her. But, watching herself on video like that, running madly through the forest, Brin saw something James couldn't have seen.

Fear.

And panic.

To a degree that was not like Brin at all.

James might have seen the fear and panic on her face, but he didn't know Brin well enough to know that she wasn't the type to get spooked by a snapping twig or the sudden flight of a bird. Something happened to get Brin running like that.

Something bad.

And it must have been really bad for her to completely miss seeing a huge ridge right in front of her and go head-first over the edge.

She remembered her dream and shivered in her chair, rubbing both arms with her hands. A man. A dragon. The man was bald. Or really short hair. A light beard that came down to his neck. That's where the dragon lived.

Brin shook her head, frustrated with herself that she

52

couldn't remember. A dragon living on the man's neck? That was nonsense, just images from her nightmare mixing with her concussed brain.

"What's the matter?" asked James.

Brin shook her head again.

"Nothing," she said. "Just can't remember what I was running from."

"Has anything come back?"

Brin sighed. "Not really."

"Well, give it time," James said.

The look on his face seemed sincerely concerned.

"Your memory should come back soon as the swelling in your brain subsides," he said.

Brin nodded slowly. He was a nice guy. Maybe that's what made him seem so weird. Brin didn't know many nice guys anymore. All the guys she knew now were self-absorbed pricks.

She looked James over. Full body scan. He wore hiking boots that were definitely broken in, scuffed leather bulging in spots to conform to James' feet. Jeans that were not so tight as to be pretentious, but not so loose that they didn't spark Brin's imagi-nation. And something else a bit lower down.

On top, James wore a light henley that conformed to his chest fairly closely. Brin was surprised at how much definition James had in his chest. She could see well-formed pectorals and even a hint of some stomach muscles under the shirt. Could it be that the nerdy weirdo had a hot body to go along with the hot face?

He pulled on a nylon puffball jacket and zipped it up, covering his chest and jarring Brin from her thoughts.

"Come on," James said. "I put your jacket in the closet by the front door."

"Wait," said Brin. "There's a video missing."

James stuffed his hands into the pockets of his jacket and avoided eye contact with Brin.

"I don't know what you mean," he said. "All the videos are there."

James was a terrible liar. That was good to know.

And, oddly, a comfort to Brin. Especially after the lying sack of bimbos that was her last boyfriend.

"I want to see the video of my fall," Brin said.

James shook his head slightly and bit his lower lip, still avoiding eye contact.

"I know you have it, James. You've got every inch of this place on video."

James threw his head back in frustration and stared at the ceiling.

He really didn't want Brin to see this video. Why? Did he do something pervy while Brin was unconscious? Other than stripping her naked and hooking her up to all sorts of medical devices?

There were a lot of things he could have done that were a lot pervier than that. But it seemed out of character for James. At least, for what little Brin knew and could sense about him.

James finally finished his silent tantrum and met Brin's eyes. Brin just looked at him, cool as a cucumber. If he wanted to throw a hissy fit, he was welcome to it. When he was done, Brin would still be waiting to watch the video.

She just arched one eyebrow at him.

"Fine," James huffed, "though why you would want to watch yourself get hurt, I have no idea."

He shouldered Brin away from the keyboard. His fingers flashed over the keys so quickly that Brin couldn't even see which keys he was pressing. The keyboard clattered like a thousand chittering bugs.

James made one final thundering whack on the enter key and two videos came up, each filling half of the the screen. The view on the left was from a high vantage point, probably in a tree, looking toward the edge of the ridge from on top. The view on the right was looking in at a door to the house. The door was solid wood and looked weathered and scarred, like it had been there for centuries. The camera angle was about waist-high, looking in at the door from the outside.

The door was partly recessed within some kind of stone cave, almost fully in shadow in the morning sun. But, the landing, made of bare rock, was visible in front, the morning dew still glistening on the stone.

Both videos were paused. James, still arched over the keyboard, looked over his shoulder at Brin.

"Are you absolutely certain you want to watch this?" he asked. "It's... quite graphic."

A sudden chill went down Brin's spine. To be honest, she wasn't sure why she wanted to watch the video. Just to fill a nagging hole in her memory, she supposed. To know exactly what went down to give her a broken leg, a hell of a headache, and a really weird story to tell.

If she ever made it out of here.

"Just play the fucking video," she said, staring James in the eye.

James held her gaze a moment longer, just enough to make Brin break eye contact and look back at the monitor.

She was nervous. Silly, but she was. Just a little bit.

James hit the spacebar and the videos started playing. There was no movement, at first. Brin wasn't sure if he'd actually started the videos. On the left, she saw only twenty feet or so of forest, a couple feet of bare rock, then blue sky. On the right, just a door with rock all around it. The resolution of the video was crystal clear, but there was no movement whatsoever.

She heard the crunch of footsteps running over wet leaves and undergrowth. Snapping twigs. She hadn't even realized the videos had sound.

Her bright red Patagonia jacket flashed into view on the left. Just as she entered the frame, Brin watched herself turn to look behind, over her shoulder. The same fear and panic she had seen in another video was splayed across her face. She kept running forward, kept looking backward.

Five steps from the edge.

Three steps.

One step.

Brin's muscles tensed involuntarily as she watched. In her mind, she was willing her on-screen self to look forward. To pay attention. To stop running, for fuck's sake.

She didn't.

She took one final step into empty blue sky.

For a split-second before her head swung forward again, Brin could see the fear and panic on her face turn to surprise and a completely different kind of fear. Where the former fear had looked like a fear born in her mind, this new fear looked like one born in the present moment. It had an urgency to it that hadn't been there before.

And then she was gone, dropped out of the bottom of the frame.

A split-second later, she appeared from the top of the frame on the right. A red blur, arms flung to the sides. The leg that had been reaching forward for her next stride was still reaching forward as she pedaled for some kind of purchase. Only now it was pointing down. Brin watched it meet the stone and snap backward and to one side, not at her knee, but midway up her shin.

She shuddered as she watched. It happened in a fraction of a second, but Brin saw it like it was in slow motion.

And that wasn't the worst of it.

The rest of Brin's body followed, folding the broken leg over itself. Her arms bent naturally at the elbow, but didn't do anything to break her fall.

That honor went to her face.

The top of her forehead, just above her hairline, met the

stone landing with shocking force. Brin's neck twisted for an instant at such a strange angle that she was amazed she hadn't suffered any spinal damage, or even any neck pain.

The rest of her body met the ground and bounced back just a bit before settling in a floppy, unconscious heap in front of James' door. If it hadn't been for her leg slowing her momentum just enough, Brin likely would have broken her skull in the fall. Or worse, she would have died.

Brin sat back in her chair. Her palms hurt. She looked down and realized that she was clenching her fists, digging her fingernails into her palms hard enough to sting, her fingers flushed red and white from the pressure.

The video continued, silent, with no movement for a few seconds.

Then, James flung open the door, shock on his blood-drained face. He turned behind him into the shadows inside the house and came back with a backboard and a neck brace. He set those down on the stone landing and very carefully moved around Brin, pressing against her spine, then examining her head before gently, ever so gently, slipping the neck brace around her neck without moving her body any more than absolutely necessary.

Once the brace was secure, he set the backboard beside Brin's body and carefully rolled her onto the board, supporting her back with one hand and rolling her body with the other. He made sure Brin's arms and legs were situated safely, then strapped her down to the board.

He dashed back into the house and returned an instant later with a gurney, pressed a button with his foot and collapsed the gurney's legs until it rested only a few inches above the ground. Carefully, using the backboard, starting with Brin's head and moving to her feet, James swiveled and slid her onto the gurney. He pulled the gurney straps over Brin and the backboard, securing her, then wheeled her into the house.

The movements were so gentle, so considerate. But the look on James' face in the video was absolutely stricken. Focused on the task at hand, but clearly worried.

James tapped the spacebar again to stop the videos.

"Do I need to show you the footage from the sickbay, too?" he said.

Did he just call it a sickbay? Brin smiled slightly, but decided not to needle James about that. After the tenderness she'd just witnessed in the video, he'd earned at least that much.

"Maybe later," she said.

James snorted.

Brin stared at the monitor, showing empty forest at the ridgetop and an empty landing in front of the door.

James was right. That video was graphic.

But, at least it had helped Brin get that dream out of her head.

"How about that walk now?" she said.

12

JAMES REALLY DIDN'T UNDERSTAND why Brin had asked to watch the video of her accident. Maybe she didn't trust him and wanted to see what he did, what medical procedures he used. But, she didn't ask to see the sickbay video, so that seemed unlikely.

Maybe she was looking for clues to jog her memory, to figure out why she'd been running in the first place. James had already scrubbed the video and seen nothing, but maybe she wanted to check for herself. That was fair.

Or, maybe she was just one of those people with a morbid curiosity. The type who slowed to a crawl whenever they passed a motor vehicle accident on the highway, hoping to catch a glimpse of a broken bone or blood on the pavement. James had never been one of those people. He hated to watch other people suffer. He didn't even really enjoy humor that came at the expense of others. To James, the Three Stooges wasn't comedy. It was an allegory for everything that was wrong with humanity.

But, maybe Brin didn't share that point of view. She certainly wouldn't be alone if she didn't. It was just one more way that James was an outsider among his own species.

But, still, even the morbidly curious tended to avoid

watching themselves suffer. The enjoyment came from the observation of suffering, not the experience. Observing oneself suffer, while removed from the present, still hit a bit too close to home for most people.

It certainly did for James. He'd watched the video several times, even going frame by frame through the actual impact, looking for the exact cause of the injuries so he could better assess and treat them. But it had made him sick to do it. Almost literally. He'd choked back his breakfast more than once during the process.

So, watching the video yet again had been an annoyance and a torment. Instead, James had watched Brin as she watched it. Her green eyes wide in the shifting light from the screen. The color in her face flushing as she approached the ridge, then draining as she landed in front of the doorway. Her body shifting in her seat, tensing and releasing throughout the video.

And yet, she did not cry out. Did not cower. Did not vomit or look away.

She was brave. That was certain. Braver than James.

And strong. James still couldn't believe she was out of bed. If he'd suffered the fall Brin had taken, he'd be in bed for a week before he even bothered to consider getting up.

Yet, here she was. Cast and crutches, ready to go for a walk outside.

Unbelievable.

And probably inadvisable.

But, James had just about given up trying to tell Brin what to do. It didn't seem to have much effect.

He grabbed Brin's coat from the closet by the front door. She looked at it for a long moment, bright red in James' hand, before James helped her pull it on.

James had altered the building site to place the house on a man-made plateau built into the face of the slope. As a result, the grade outside the door descended fairly gently for the first twenty feet or so before dropping off more steeply as it blended back into the natural slope of the mountain. That plateau ran the length of the front of the house before ending against the hard shoulder of the ridge.

Brin moved carefully over the uneven ground, James close by her side in case she stumbled. She moved slowly, but smoothly and without incident. James took her straight out from the door and turned around to show her the ridge from which she'd fallen.

"Woah," said Brin under her breath.

"It's a long way to fall," said James. "Twenty-two feet from the peak, where you went over." He could tell from the expression on her face that Brin was fully aware of just how lucky she was to be standing more or less in one piece just a day after falling from that height onto bare rock.

The house had been dug into the ridge, extending for about a hundred feet straight into the hill, then down three stories underground. One of the contractors had said it was like a German pillbox in World War II. James liked to think of it more like a hobbit house from Lord of the Rings.

Either way, it was well-hidden. And James intended to keep it that way.

"You see," said James, pointing along the ridge above the house, "the ridge extends over the length of the house and continues on for a half mile in one direction and a quarter mile in the other direction. There are spots where you can free climb it, but not in your condition."

Brin nodded, then turned around to look down the slope in the other direction. That maneuver alone required several movements of her crutches.

"And that slope doesn't look too friendly, either," she said.

James nodded. "It's manageable, but not with crutches."

"I could slide down on my butt, maybe?" said Brin.

"You shouldn't even be walking on crutches yet," said James, "and now you want to toboggan down a mountain without a sled?"

"Could use that backboard."

"We're not discussing this."

"The one from the video that you strapped me to?"

"Brin."

"You can strap me to it again and drag me down."

"Okay, I'm going back inside now."

James turned back toward the front door.

"We'd be like Eskimos," Brin called after him, "or sled dogs."

James kept walking.

"You'd be the dog, of course."

James went inside the house.

"Heel, James!" he heard Brin call through the open door. "Bad dog!"

James couldn't help but smile.

13

BRIN HAD BEEN JOKING about tobogganing down the mountain, but only half-joking. She was no longer worried for her own safety. Not from James, anyway. He didn't seem like the type to take advantage of a woman.

Of course, that's how all the serial killers seem.

Still, Brin didn't get that feeling from James, at all. He was definitely a weirdo, but he was also sweet, in a nerdy, anxious way.

She wasn't worried about James taking advantage of her, but she was worried about her medical care. Her leg felt fine. Surprisingly so, actually. James was right. She shouldn't be walking around, even on crutches, so soon after a fall like she'd taken. But she'd been walking around all day and suffered no ill effects, aside from slight fatigue and very sore armpits.

And her headaches, so painful just yesterday, were now only a dull throb in the background.

But, what if she threw a blood clot? What if she got an infection? What if her headaches came back?

Or—what really concerned her—what if her memories didn't?

As kind as James had been, as incredibly well-stocked his

bizarre basement was, medically, it wasn't safe for Brin to be here with no way out. No way to get to a hospital. No way for them to come to her. No way to call for help.

Jesus.

Brin couldn't believe she hadn't thought of it before.

"James?" she called as she swung her way through the house on her crutches.

She found James in that odd room with the machines in different-sized boxes. He had the door open on one of the large boxes and was squatting down behind it, tinkering with something inside. He poked his head around the door when he heard her come in.

He was wearing glasses. Rectangular, tortoise-shell glasses that made his eyes appear huge when he looked at her.

Brin's heart skipped for a second.

Brin loved the nerdy glasses look on guys. She'd never dated anyone with that look. She'd just never had the opportunity. But, it had always gotten her pulse racing.

Just as it did now.

James arched his eyebrows, waiting. A strand of his long, dark hair fell over his forehead.

That only made it worse.

"Yes, Brin?" James asked. "Everything ok?"

"Um..."

She sounded like an idiot. She shook her head quickly to snap herself back to reality.

"Yeah," she said. She struggled for a moment to reboard the train of thought she'd ridden in on. "Um... cell phone."

"Cell phone," replied James, clearly needing something more to go on.

"My cell phone," said Brin. "Do you know where it is?"

"Oh, shit," said James, standing quickly, setting down the screwdriver he'd been holding—and, unfortunately, his glasses—on a shelf as he went into the adjoining office. He was in there for a few minutes. Brin could hear him opening and closing drawers and muttering softly to himself.

James came back with a clear plastic Ziploc bag. He pulled Brin's cell phone out and handed her the phone and the bag.

"Thanks," she said.

"Sorry," said James. "That's everything you had on you when you fell. I should have given it to you earlier, but with everything going on, I forgot I had it all."

"It's okay," said Brin.

She looked through the plastic at the contents of the bag. Her driver's license was in there, along with some lip balm, a small tube of sunscreen, a half-empty roll of Mentos, and her car keys. She'd forgotten all about her car. It had only been what, two days? She'd parked in a public lot with no charge. Hopefully, it hadn't been marked as abandoned. They wouldn't do that after only two days, right?

James had been saying something, but Brin hadn't been listening.

"What?" she asked.

"Your cell phone," he said, pointing at it with the screwdriver he'd just picked up. "There's no signal up here. Won't do you much good."

Brin checked her phone. The battery was down to twenty percent and she had no cell signal at all.

Shit. So much for letting her friends know she was ok. They were probably freaking out right now.

"What about wi-fi?" Brin asked. "Can I get your password?"

James put his glasses back on and ducked back behind the door to the machine.

"No, sorry," he said, his voice muffled a bit. "Everything's hard-wired here. No wi-fi."

Brin checked her phone. He was right. No wi-fi icon, either. That was weird, even for James. All of that high-tech shit he had in the house, and no wi-fi?

"What about the cameras?" she asked.

"What about them?"

"They're all wireless, aren't they?"

James sighed and sat back on his heels to look at Brin from around the door to the machine. He pulled his glasses, those delicious glasses, down to the tip of his nose and looked over them at her.

"Just because the cameras are wireless, doesn't mean I have wi-fi that you can use with your cell phone."

He said it like he was talking to a particularly dense seven-year-old.

It really got on Brin's nerves.

"They all come into a wireless receiver," James continued, "but it's only for the cameras. It's not connected to the internet."

"Right," Brin said. "So you're out here in the middle of nowhere all by yourself in an impassable forest with no internet and no means of communication with the outside world? How do you order food and medicine and more..." She waved toward the machine James was using. "...shit for your... toys."

James started to say something, but seemed to think better of it. Just as well. Brin was frustrated and ready for a fight.

"I'm sorry your cell phone doesn't work here, Brin," he said softly. "I am."

And she believed him.

That fucker.

Him and his hot glasses.

Brin blew out a breath of deep frustration. She was fucked. How long until she'd be able to walk without crutches? Six weeks? More?

She couldn't stay here that long. She had friends. Family too, though they were unlikely to notice if she didn't contact them for six weeks.

And her job. She'd probably lose that if she couldn't at least call in to explain herself.

James finished whatever he was doing with the machine, stood up, and closed the door. He fiddled with something on the touchscreen attached to the side of the box. It whirred to life. Brin could see a large block of some kind of material inside. The metal arm swung toward it with some kind of spinning knife attached and started cutting away at the block.

"What is that thing, anyway?" asked Brin.

"It's a CNC machine."

"What does it do?"

"I can design objects in three dimensions on my computer and this machine will make them for me."

Brin nodded. So it was a manufacturing machine.

She gestured toward the other machines around the room. "Are all of these other things CNC machines, too?"

"Some of them. Others, the smaller ones, plus this big one here," he pointed to the other large machine in the room, "are 3-D printers."

"What do they do?"

"Same basic principle," said James, "except where CNC machines remove material from a starting block to make the object, 3-D printers build objects by adding layers of material on top of each other."

"Makes sense," nodded Brin.

"Does it?" James was looking at her in a weird way, smiling. Brin had a sinking feeling there was some mansplaining about to happen.

That would not do.

"Yeah, it does, James," Brin said. "You may find it hard to believe, but even a poor crippled woman like me can understand the principle of using a machine to build shit."

James looked as stunned as if Brin had slapped him.

Okay, maybe that was a little unfair, but Brin was still pissed —and worried—about her cell phone not working. And that was James' fault. Who the fuck doesn't have internet access these days?

"I'm sorry," stammered James. "I didn't mean to–"

"Yeah," said Brin. "I know."

Taking her anger out on James didn't make her feel better at all.

In fact, it only made her feel angrier.

At herself.

14

J AMES WATCHED the metal arm of the CNC machine move smoothly and efficiently along the path he had programmed for it. The router slowly carved away areas from the carbon fiber substrate. James loved to watch the machine at work. To watch the object slowly take shape as extraneous material was removed. And the whirring and humming sound of the router always soothed James' nerves.

Until now.

James really didn't know what he'd said to make Brin so angry at him. She'd suddenly gotten very short with him and stormed out of the room.

As much as anyone can storm out of a room when they're on crutches.

Maybe she sensed his lie.

He was pretty sure she didn't pick up on it outright. Her facial expression was just confused, not suspicious, when he made up the lie about the wi-fi. But he was pretty sure she didn't really buy it. Not completely.

And he was pretty sure that's what had really made her angry.

Although, he could see how she might have misinterpreted

69

his question. It just wasn't often that he met anyone who even tried to understand why he used the CNC machines and 3-D printers. Most people in the past had simply wondered why he didn't just buy what he needed, pre-made. Or hire someone to make it for him. He had the money, after all. Why waste it on expensive machines and materials when it just meant more work for him? It was a reasonable question for wealthy, privileged people in a consumer culture to ask.

He just didn't want to be like that anymore.

He wanted the ability to take an idea from his head and, with a little bit of honest effort, hold it in his hands a few hours or days later. It was his favorite feeling these days. He didn't need contracts or negotiations or service-level agreements. He just needed patience, time, and some raw materials.

Just as he was doing now. He'd had an idea, created a 3-D model on his computer, converted that model into instructions for the CNC machine, and now was watching his idea become a reality.

It was a beautiful, creative, peaceful process. He would be happy to spend the rest of his life alone in the mountains "building shit", as Brin had put it.

Which is exactly why he'd switched off the wi-fi when he was getting her phone. Cell phones meant communication. Communication meant curious people would come looking for her. Curious people meant James' quiet life in the woods was over.

He did feel bad about it, but not too much. Brin was in no danger. Her leg was clearly doing fine, as was her concussion. Her memory would return soon enough.

And James had come up with a plan for getting her out of there.

And it had started with Brin's idea.

The backboard.

She'd been joking, but it was actually a decent idea.

Okay, not by itself. Dragging her down the mountain strapped to a backboard would only result in injuries for both of them.

But, if he strapped her to the gurney, using the backboard as extra support, he could do it. He'd have to beef up the tires, but the legs were already designed to handle uneven surfaces with minimal disturbance to the patient.

It would look a little strange and suspicious if anyone saw him wheeling a woman on a stretcher through the woods, but James felt sure he could avoid being seen.

He just needed to make sure Brin herself didn't see anything. He didn't want her to be able to find his house again, or tell anyone else how to find it.

He needed her to be unconscious.

And that part of the plan did make him feel bad. James didn't use drugs and rarely drank. The idea of dosing someone when they didn't medically need it ran counter to his principles. It felt wrong. It felt nefarious. His reasons made sense and his intentions were as honorable as they could be, under the circumstances, but it still felt wrong to him.

He just couldn't think of a better idea.

And time was running out.

Brin had already been gone more than twenty-four hours. People would get worried soon. They might call the police.

And then things could get complicated.

And "complicated" was exactly what James did not want. He'd had enough "complicated" for a lifetime.

He needed a plan. Now.

He already had the mode of transport: the gurney. Next, he needed to scout a path down the mountain that the gurney could manage with no risk of tipping or toppling or otherwise jeopardizing Brin's safety. He had a route in mind, but needed to double-check to make sure it was viable.

He already had the means to render Brin unconscious. He

had enough flunitrazepam on hand to do the job. Normally used to assist with anesthesia, it was somewhat risky, but he already knew Brin's exact weight and had some sense of how quickly she metabolized medication from the pain meds he'd given her when she first arrived. That minimized the risk considerably.

He just needed the method of delivery. It was unlikely he could get her to swallow a pill. He should have established a regular pill-taking regimen from the start, but it was too late for that now. He really had not expected her to be mobile so quickly. He'd figured he had at least three days with Brin being bedridden. In that state, it would be trivial for him to maintain an IV and slip her an appropriate dose when the time was right.

Her stubborn and remarkable good health was making James' life more difficult.

And the IV option was clearly no longer viable. There was no way James would be able to convince Brin to submit to an IV now. That left only two options: injection or oral liquids.

Despite the casual way spy movies depicted injections as a quick stick in the neck that knocked out the recipient almost immediately, James had little confidence that a) he could sneak up on Brin and inject her vein quickly and cleanly, or b) the flunitrazepam would take effect quickly enough to prevent her from retaliating or fleeing. And the last thing James wanted was for Brin to be alone in the woods passed out from Rohypnol. He could never live with himself then.

That left oral liquid as the delivery mechanism of choice.

He would spike her drink.

Just like every date rapist on the planet.

James' skin crawled at the thought, but he forced himself to focus on the broader goal. He would get Brin back to civilization without compromising either her safety or his isolation.

But what would he do then? He couldn't very well just leave her on the side of the road. He would need some way to ensure she was found without revealing himself. Perhaps he could sneak her into a hospital or drop her in front of a firehouse or police station.

But those locations would most likely be in heavily trafficked areas. They would also probably have robust surveillance. No, he'd have to drop her in a remote location and have the authorities come to her.

He could take her to his usual delivery drop zone, but he didn't want to leave any connection to himself. The flunitrazepam would leave her with some retrograde amnesia. She already had some of that from her concussion. The cast on her leg and her memory of her time with James would certainly be a inconvenient problem, but there was nothing to be done about that now. The authorities knew he was in the area, but had no reason to seek him out. Restoring a woman to health was not a crime.

But drugging her against her will would be.

He would have to wait until the dose wore off before turning her over. He would have to calibrate the dose very carefully so that she would be unconscious long enough for James to get her down the mountain to a drop zone, but not so long that he had to wait forever for her to wake up.

And he didn't want her to wake up before medical personnel arrived. He didn't want her wandering around, getting lost or hurt.

This would be tricky, especially with an oral dose. He had to make sure she drank enough to knock her out, but not so much that she stayed unconscious too long.

James was beginning to regret helping Brin in the first place. In retrospect, he should have dragged her down the mountain and called 9-1-1 right away instead of bringing her in and fixing her up himself.

But that had been too risky. He'd thought of that at the time and decided he didn't want to be responsible for hurting Brin even more—or even killing her—on the way down the mountain.

So he'd taken her in, assuming he could find a way to get rid of her safely once he knew she was stable. But, her injuries were not as severe as it seemed they should have been from the nature of the fall. And now she was mobile and James was left to concoct a dastardly scheme worthy of any movie villain.

How had he become the villain here? He'd only been trying to help.

James sighed.

This is why it was better just to avoid people altogether.

"James?"

Brin was standing in the doorway.

She'd come back.

"I... just want to apologize," she said, quietly. "For going off on you earlier."

"Oh," replied James. Brin looked very uncomfortable. James got the sense she didn't apologize much. "It's okay, really."

"Thanks, but it's really not okay." She was rubbing one arm nervously and looking everywhere but at James. "You've been nothing but kind and helpful to me since my... accident. I'm just frustrated with the whole situation. But, I have no right to take it out on you."

"Hey, listen," said James, moving to stand before Brin.

She finally lifted her eyes to his.

"Don't be so hard on yourself," James continued. "I can't even begin to imagine what you're going through. Between the fall and the injuries and the amnesia."

It really was a lot. If James were in Brin's place, he'd be freaking out.

"Maybe you should go back and lie down a bit more," he continued. "You might be pushing yourself too hard too soon."

The fact that doing so would make it much easier for James to put his plan in motion was just a bonus. He really did think

Brin should lie down again and get back on the IV. She probably still needed more fluids.

"Thanks, James," said Brin.

She rested a hand on James' arm. It was a friendly gesture, a gesture of gratitude and goodwill. It also sent electric shockwaves through James' entire body. His face felt flushed and Brin's face suddenly seemed hazy before him, softer, like a photograph under soft light. Her limpid green eyes that made him want to dive in and never come up for air. Her long, silky red hair that somehow looked amazing after a dangerous fall and two days in a hospital bed.

James had been close to Brin before, but always in a medical capacity. This was the first time he'd been this close to her when she was conscious and under her own strength. He'd noticed her brilliant eyes and striking hair the first time he saw her on the surveillance camera, but he'd never noticed the light freckles dusting the tops of her cheeks. He'd never noticed the milky smoothness of her skin. He'd never noticed the way she smelled like cinnamon and... cherries? How could she possibly smell so good after two days in a hospital bed?

James saw Brin's cheeks burn bright red. She quickly dropped her hand from his arm.

He must have been staring. He was gawking at her like a little boy and she'd noticed and been put off by it.

"Um..." she said, glancing down at the floor, "let me do something to pay you back, at least a little."

"You really don't need to."

"How about I make you dinner? Tonight?"

"No, really."

"Come on. We gotta eat, right?"

James had an idea.

He hated hiself for it, but he had an idea.

"Actually, you made me breakfast this morning," he said, "so I'm going to make you dinner tonight."

"How does that help me pay you back?"

James grinned. "It doesn't. But you shouldn't be making dinner for anyone right now. You've already been up and about far too much."

"I'm fine, James. You don't need to–"

James held up a hand to cut her off. "Please," he said. "I may not be a doctor, but I'm the best thing you've got right now. Let me finish the job."

Brin seemed about to protest again, but James gave her a stern look. She sighed and her shoulders slumped.

Victory.

"Fine," said Brin. "But I will make you dinner at some point."

"And I'll hold you to that," James replied, "but, for now, please sit down, lay down, do something to rest, okay?"

As he watched Brin click away on her crutches, James mind raced ahead. About three hours until dinner.

Three hours to put his plan together.

15

Brin had been more tired than she thought.

With no real intention of sleeping, she had hobbled back downstairs on her crutches mainly to appease James. She figured she could humor him and lay down for half an hour or so, long enough to claim she'd tried, then get back up.

But, she had closed her eyes and didn't open them again until three-and-a-half hours later.

Groggy from the long nap, she swung her legs off the bed in the dark downstairs room. James had moved the monitors and the IV pole back into storage in the adjoining room, giving Brin more space. It made the room feel more like a bedroom instead of a hospital.

James still didn't want her to move to an actual bedroom upstairs yet, in case something went south and she needed medical care in a hurry. Brin didn't know what could go south at this point, and James didn't elaborate. But, she played along for the time being. It was his house, after all. He could put her wherever he wanted.

Brin rolled her shoulders up, down, and around, then made wide circles with her neck, trying to stretch out her muscles. The movements were painful, but not as painful as the constant soreness she felt. She shouldn't be surprised, after the fall she'd taken. The human neck just wasn't made to bend the way it had in that video. Once again, Brin felt lucky just to be alive and fully functioning. She could—and maybe should—be dead or paralyzed.

Still, Brin had never been a patient woman, least of all when it came to her own healing. She wanted to be up and about as soon as she could get away with it. Rest and recuperation be damned.

The stretching felt good. Felt like she'd gotten blood flowing to parts of her muscles that hadn't had it in a while. As she grabbed her crutches from the side of her bed and pushed to a standing position, she wished she could stand on both feet, just for a little while, and do a full-body stretch. Stretch out her back, her spine. Get a good stretch on her quads and hamstrings. Her whole body just felt wound up tight, blocked and knotted throughout.

She'd have to ask James if he had a hot tub or at least a bathtub where she could have a hot soak for a while. Something to try to ease the tension in her muscles.

Maybe he would even agree to give her a massage.

Brin let herself soak in that thought for a few seconds. Her nude body face-down on the bed with James straddling her, rubbing warm oil all across her back. The heater in the room would be on, a light sweat on their skin. James would get warm from the room and the exertion and ask politely if Brin minded if he took off his own shirt, just to cool off for a while.

Of course she didn't mind.

Brin smiled and shook the thought from her head.

What would it be like to date a kind man, a smart and caring man? Brin had never had that before. She'd only dated horny jocks and self-centered artists. She couldn't even imagine dating someone who was actually good for her. The very idea felt wrong, completely foreign.

That was probably not a healthy state of mind to live in.

Brin managed, far too slowly for her own liking, to get upstairs. The smell greeted her before she heard the sizzle of the pan. It smelled incredible, like butter and garlic and hot bread. When she got into the kitchen, she saw James standing at the stove, a Viking grill with six gas burners. He was wearing an apron over a white button-down shirt tucked neatly into dark grey dress pants. He looked like they could be headed out on an actual date at a real restaurant.

Except for the fact that his feet were bare.

"I didn't know I was supposed to dress up," Brin said from the doorway. "I would have worn my sweater."

James looked over his shoulder at her and smiled.

Brin couldn't help but think about that massage again. It was lucky she was using crutches or she might have fallen down right there.

"There are clothes you can try in my bedroom, if you want," he said. He gestured with his head. "Down the hall, third door on the right. First closet on the left."

That was a first. Brin had never had a guy try to put clothes *on* her before when they were on a date. Too often they could think about nothing but getting her clothes off.

Brin couldn't decide if she was impressed or offended.

She clicked down the hallway on her crutches. The left wall was solid, with several doors along the right. She passed a small workout room with an elliptical, a treadmill, and some body-weight devices. The next room was another small office, with an armchair, a small desk, and a bookshelf that ran the length of one wall.

The third door was the bedroom. Brin entered slowly. There was a hallway in front of her, with a door to the left and another to the right. Both doors were open. They opened onto massive closets, each big enough to be a small bedroom, each with a large dresser-valet combination in the center.

As far as Brin could see, the closets and the bedroom were floored in thick shag carpet that welcomed Brin's feet in a soft embrace and swallowed entirely the sound of her crutches.

The closet to the right was only a quarter full. What clothes were there were hung neatly or folded meticulously on a series of shelves that ran along the walls under the hanging clothes. Men's shirts and pants, suit jackets, sweaters and jeans. That had to be James' closet.

Brin turned to the closet on her left and swung herself inside.

As large as the closet was, it was full to the point where it almost seemed too small for the clothing there. There were women's dresses of every color, pattern and cut from light, breezy summer dresses to evening gowns. Racks of women's shoes in a variety of styles, from practical, comfortable sneakers to high-heeled shoes in wild colors to tall leather boots with buckles and zippers and laces. Sweaters and pants and blouses and skirts and comfortable joggers and pajamas, all arrayed around the room in a dizzying assortment. The center dresser had all manner of jewelry piled on it. Brin opened a few drawers and found underwear and stockings and slips and the like.

It was any woman's dream closet.

But all of the clothes seemed brand new. Many still had the tags on them.

And why the hell would James have a closet full of brand new women's clothes in his remote house in the woods?

Brin wondered again what she had fallen into when she landed on James' doorstep. There was definitely more here than just a hot, nerdy, unusually well-prepared guy bending over backwards to help an injured person in need.

She mused over these thoughts as she scanned the room looking for something nice to wear. It felt odd enough getting dressed up for a dinner at home. It felt even more odd to do so with a guy she just met, in his house, while on crutches from a horrific fall the day before. But, somehow, the oddest of all was browsing through these clothes that seemed so beautiful and so strangely out of place here.

Brin had never been a fashionista, nor had she ever been one of those girls who would swoon over a pair of shoes or a beautiful outfit. But, she did appreciate beautiful clothes when she saw them. And she did like the feeling of being dressed to impress, and turning heads as a result.

She wanted to wear something nice, something sexy, but not slutty. She wanted to see if she could get James' mind working, see if he responded at all.

But, of course, the leg cast and the crutches put a snag in the usual options.

She scanned past the evening gowns (too difficult to maneuver) and the summer dresses (too short and too cold) and the pant suits (too stuffy and impossible to wear with a cast). She was beginning to think she'd be stuck with sweatpants and an old sweater until she found one dress tucked at the end of a row. It was a simple, sleeveless black dress, close-fitting, but tasteful, that came down to just above Brin's knees, leaving plenty of room for the cast.

She found a beautiful lace embroidery stole in a lovely gold shade that would offset her hair color and suit the dress perfectly. And it would help keep her arms and shoulders warm.

It took a little doing, but Brin managed to get the dress on and zipped while standing on one foot. She pulled on the stole and examined the look in the full-length three-way mirror that stood in the center of one wall.

Even with the crutches and the cast, Brin liked what she saw. The dress hugged the curves of her athletic body in all the right places without bunching or sagging. Whoever had bought this dress must have had a build similar to Brin's. The stole added a touch of elegance and finish to the outfit and it did, indeed, offset Brin's hair color beautifully.

Unfortunately, the hair itself was a disaster.

It looked just like Brin had run madly through the woods, fallen twenty feet onto her head, and lay unconscious in a hospital bed for a day.

It would not do for a dinner date.

Brin noticed a door in the corner of the room that she had not seen before. It led to a large bathroom with a deep free-standing tub, an open shower, and a long vanity with a makeup station. It was one of those setups like you'd see in a theater dressing room, with the rows of lights running up one side of a wide mirror, across the top, and down the other side.

Like the closet, this station seemed fully stocked with makeup, hairbrushes, and product, all seemingly unused.

Brin moved over and set herself down in the comfortable leather swivel chair in front of the mirror, resting her crutches against the counter. She didn't want to wash her hair. It would take too long to dry. So, she sprayed it with some detangler and set to work on it with a brush. After a few minutes of playing tug-of-war, the knots and snags finally started working out and she could run the brush through her hair without feeling like she was pulling clumps of hair out of her head. A few minutes more and her hair was feeling almost normal again.

Brin had never been much for wearing makeup. She'd been blessed with clear, fair skin and a natural glow. At least, that's what her friends told her, usually with pouty expressions on their faces. Brin had just never seen the point of spending an hour each day painting your face just so you could leave the house.

But, that didn't mean she was above using a bit of makeup here and there. On special occasions. Just a light dusting of foundation, a touch of eye shadow, and a subtle lipstick were plenty.

When Brin had applied the makeup and decided her look was about as good as it was going to get under the circumstances, she lifted herself back up onto her crutches. She turned to go back through the door to the closet, but noticed a second door on the opposite wall. She swung herself over there and tried the handle. The door opened easily, swinging outward into a large bedroom with a king-size bed, two nightstands, and a fireplace with a thick shag throw rug over a tile floor in front of it.

Across the hallway to Brin's right was a door similar to the one she had just opened. Brin assumed it led to a bathroom like the one she'd been in, and from there into James' closet.

It was a beautiful, cozy, comfortable bedroom.

Built for two.

On one side of the bed, the sheets were slightly crinkled like the bed had been slept in last night and made that morning. The other side was pulled tight and flat like it hadn't been used in a long time.

A king size bed with only one occupant.

What on earth was going on here, James?

Brin shook her head, then went back out the way she had come, shutting the bedroom door behind her.

"Sorry for taking so long," she said when she had made it back to the kitchen.

James had set the table with candles and fresh bread wrapped in a cloth napkin in a wicker bowl. Fresh salad was piled in a bowl beside each setting. James was hunched over the counter plating the main course from the pan.

"There was a lot to choose from," Brin continued.

"No problem," said James over his shoulder. "You're just in time."

He set the empty pan back on the stove and returned to fussing over the plates. He looked like a master chef on a cooking show perfecting his plating.

"I have a special treat for dessert," James said without looking at Brin.

"Wow, dessert, too?"

"Well, a dessert wine. Have you ever had port?"

"Port?" said Brin. "Nope. Never. Now you're just spoiling me."

James laughed. "You should taste the food before you say that."

He grabbed the two plates, one in each hand. As he turned toward her, he said, "I hope you like..."

His voice trailed off and his face went slack as he took in her appearance before meeting Brin's eyes.

"...scallops," he finished in a whisper.

Brin smiled.

"I love them," she said.

16

James had surprised himself when he'd offered a fresh change of clothes for Brin. He'd stewed about it for a while after she left, distracting himself enough to overcook the first pan of scallops. Fortunately, he had more, and scallops don't take long to cook.

The idea of someone else wearing Carrie's clothes seemed wrong to him. At least, intellectually it did. And yet, the offer he'd made to Brin had slipped out as quickly and easily as if it was the most natural and obvious thing in the world.

And it felt right.

That was what had confused him enough to burn the first batch of scallops. His brain was saying one thing, but his feelings were telling him something completely different.

That didn't happen to James very often.

In fact, he couldn't recall the last time it had happened.

It had thrown him for a loop for a few minutes while he struggled to process that misalignment. He'd finally pulled himself together enough to finish the meal and plate it when he turned and saw Brin.

Wearing Carrie's favorite dress.

The dress Carrie had worn on their first date together.

The dress James had taken off her months later when they first made love.

The dress she'd been wearing that beautiful night in Hawaii when she'd agreed to marry him.

And now Brin was standing in front of him. Wearing that dress, that special dress that meant so much to James.

She looked gorgous. The dress fit her like it had been made for her. The stole was a gorgous mustard color that accentuated the orange tones in her hair, which was shining warm and red in the candle glow. And her face, normally beautiful, was absolutely radiant in that light.

She was stunning.

James should have been furious.

For Brin to wear that dress was a desecration. A violation.

His mind was aghast. Incensed. Indignant.

But, his body was alive. Tingling all over.

He couldn't speak. Couldn't think straight.

He was dumbfounded.

The last time he'd felt that way was the first time he'd seen Carrie, sitting on a bench outside the conference room at a data science convention.

The day he'd fallen in love with her.

And now, here it was again.

It should have been wrong.

But it felt absolutely right.

James hid the system overload he was experiencing by serving the food and focusing on the menial tasks at hand. He set down the plates of scallops, filled their glasses with fresh water.

Brin came to the table and James pulled out her chair for her and helped her get settled.

Once he was sure everything was set, he took a deep breath and sat down opposite Brin.

"This looks incredible, James," said Brin. "I had no idea you could cook like this."

"Oh, well, I've had lots of time to practice since I moved here."

"How long have you lived here?"

"I'm sorry," said James, "that I served all of the food together like this."

He knew he was ducking her question, but he was still reeling from seeing her across the table from him, in the candlelight, wearing that dress. It was such a powerful resonance, a dejà vu, a superimposition of experiences across time and space, like a quantum entanglement, that he wasn't sure he could hold himself together if she were to start asking questions.

He was cracked open like an egg. He was liable to spill his yolk if she were to start to pry.

"I should have served one course at a time," he continued. "It would have been better that way."

"James," said Brin. She smiled, and James' mind went offline again. "This is wonderful. Incredible."

She sliced a scallop and skewered it with her fork.

"You really didn't have to do this," Brin said, bringing the scallop to her lips. She moaned with pleasure as she took it into her mouth. "But I'm so glad you did," she said.

She closed her eyes and chewed the scallop slowly, seeming to savor every bite.

"James," she said, once she'd swallowed the mouthful. "That may be the best scallop I've ever had."

It was a silly thing, a simple thing. Anyone can cook a good scallop once they learn how. But hearing Brin's effusive praise filled James with a warmth that spread through his chest. He was sure he was blushing. He just hoped it wasn't too obvious in the dim candlelight.

"I'm glad you like it," he said. "The last time I made this was for my..."

Spilling his yolk already. He caught himself.

"...for a friend," he finished, lamely.

To her credit, Brin didn't press him.

They ate slowly, savoring the food and the conversation. They talked about Brin and her childhood in Chicago, the wanderlust and frustration that had driven her West to Portland to study art at U of P, the stagnation and aimlessness that characterized the last few years for her.

Brin dreamed of being an artist, she said, of having gallery shows and living off of money earned from the sale of her work. She just shrugged when James asked why she hadn't pursued it yet.

They talked about the house and how it was built. James tried to censor his words to stop himself from imparting any details that might make the house too memorable or reveal its location. But as they talked and Brin asked questions, showing sincere interest in the answers, James found himself wanting to reveal more and more.

Finally, Brin asked the question that James knew would have to come.

"James," she said, delicately, "if it's none of my business, please just say so. But..." She paused as if debating whether or not to ask. Her curiosity must have gotten the better of her. "Why do you have all those clothes in the bedroom, and all the makeup?"

She had been kind enough to give James an easy out. He could just demur, say it was personal. He could simply say he would prefer not to talk about it. He knew Brin would accept that answer, that she would respect his privacy and not press him.

But, he was afraid that if he went down that path, he would never be able to come back. That there would forever be a barrier between them, a line that could not be crossed.

And to his surprise, he found himself wanting to answer her

honestly. He didn't want his privacy respected. He wanted it to be shared.

He'd been alone in this house in the woods for so long, working hard to avoid detection, to avoid contact with anyone at all. Yet now, in this moment, he found himself wanting to share his most painful memories with this woman who had literally fallen into his life only yesterday.

His mind could not comprehend the impulse, but it was no longer in control.

With his fork, James pushed the last few bites of linguine in brown butter sauce to the corner of his plate.

"They're not for me," James said, keeping his eyes down, then peeking up at Brin.

She laughed.

"Okay," she said. "That's good to know."

James smiled back. As he did, a barrier in his mind, in his heart finally fell. With it fell a tightness he had carried in his chest and in his mind for years and years. The release came not with the words he spoke, but with the decision he made then and there to speak them.

"I bought them for my fianceè, Carrie, three years ago."

"Oh," said Brin, sitting back in her chair. "I didn't know you were married." Despite her efforts to hide it, James could see the shock on her face.

"I'm not," said James, making eye contact with Brin and holding it. "Never was."

"Okay," said Brin slowly.

"Carrie and I met at a conference six years ago. We fell hard and fast. It was a new and unexpected experience for both of us, but we couldn't deny how we felt about each other. And neither of us wanted to."

Brin pushed aside her empty plate and leaned forward, her elbows on the table. Her brow was furrowed as she concentrated on what James was saying.

James mouth suddenly felt dry. He took a long sip of water.

"We dated for a year before moving in together," he continued. "I proposed a year after that."

He smiled at the thought. The smile slowly faded.

"She started getting tired a lot. We figured it was because she was pushing herself too hard on the wedding planning.

"Then came the headaches, brutal ones. Like migraines. They would last for hours. She would curl up in bed in the dark and just rock back and forth to get through the pain. Medicine, cold compress, neck massages. Nothing helped.

"Three months after she'd said 'yes', Carrie was diagnosed with Grade IV gliomatosis cerebri."

The words sounded so precise, so clinical, so scientific. Yet, that precision belied the abolute helplessness of modern medicine to treat the disease. Even now, those words brought the bitter taste of bile to the back of James' tongue.

Brin made a soft sound. James looked at her face and saw it contorted in concern, empathy, and compassion.

But, not pity, thankfully.

"The doctors said chemotherapy would do more harm than good. They tried a course of radiation, but it just made Carrie sick and wasn't reducing the gliomas."

James balanced his water glass on the edge of its base, rocking it back and forth on the table. It made a gentle scraping sound, back and forth.

"They gave her a year, maybe eighteen months."

"How old was she?" Brin asked softly.

"Twenty-four," James replied.

Brin just shook her head slowly.

"I started building this place," James said, looking at the room around him and, by extension, the house. "Silicon Valley was too much. Too intense. Too crowded. Too... selfish.

"I stopped working. I only worked on three things: taking

care of Carrie, building this house." He swallowed hard. His voice broke. "And finding a cure."

Why was he telling Brin all of this? Why would she care? It's just a sob story from a stranger. She probably just wants to go back downstairs and get away from the sad, weird guy.

Just then, she reached her hand across the table and grabbed James' wrist, gave it a squeeze.

He looked up, looked into her deep green eyes. He didn't see callous disregard. He didn't see a desire to get away.

He saw genuine pain. Like she'd been through it herself.

And James had to admit that it felt good to say these things out loud. He'd never told anyone his whole story before. Some people knew bits and pieces: Carrie's family. Her best friends. But no one knew the whole thing. And no one knew it from James' side.

"I threw money at both problems," he continued. "The money got the house built. Fast. Carrie and I talked about moving here, simplifying our lives. Just the two of us. I'd take care of her. We'd do research and experiments together. We'd find a cure. We'd beat it."

James shook his head. It staggered him now, in retrospect, to see his arrogance. His hubris. He had fallen prey to the delusions of the Valley, delusions that made people think that because they build some shiny piece of technology that became a hit and made them stupidly rich in no time at all they could solve any problem in the world. World hunger? Should be easy. Immortality? No problem. Homelessness? I'm free this morning.

Cancer?

I can cure that.

Give me six months.

"I stocked the house with everything I could think of that Carrie would need," James continued. "Medical supplies, of course. Diagnostic equipment, research equipment, manufacturing equipment. But, also clothing, shoes, makeup, food, books and music. Everything that Carrie loved, I made sure it was here. I wanted this to be her paradise. I wanted her to feel happy here."

James fell silent. Even knowing the end of the story, he could still feel that hope within him. He still believed he could make it happen.

"And was she?" asked Brin.

James raised a questioning eyebrow.

"Was she happy here?" Brin said.

James let go of Brin's hand and fell back in his chair.

"She never even saw this place," he said. "She died a week before we were supposed to move in."

Silence hung over the table like the moments after a tornado rips through a neighborhood. The scraps of food on the plates, the empty water glasses, the half-eaten bread were the path of destruction.

"That's a hell of a story, James," said Brin, finally. "I'm so sorry."

James nodded. It really was a hell of a story. And it was hell to live through.

"Well," he said. "Thanks for listening."

He stood and gathered the plates, brought them to the sink. Brin came up beside him carrying the bread basket and the salad bowls. James just stared down the drain of the sink.

His mind was dark and brooding. He felt lighter, having finally shared his story. But now his mind was lost, wandering the dark halls of his memory. Carrie was a whisp, an afterimage that he would see just ahead, disappearing around corners. When he'd chase her shadow, he'd arrive just in time to see it disappear around the next corner.

A house of corners in his mind.

Leading him in circles.

"Hey," said Brin.

The sound snapped James back to the present. He looked at her, standing beside him at the sink.

"How about that dessert, huh?"

James blanched.

The port.

His brilliant plan.

Earlier, he'd poured down the drain all but a glassful from a bottle that was already open. Then, he'd spiked a full, unopened second bottle, slipping a small-bore syringe through the wax and cork and injecting enough flunitrazepam to knock Brin out. You could see the tiny hole left by the needle, but only if you were looking for it.

Because port glasses were so small, James could more easily gauge the dose Brin consumed. If she drank one glass quickly, that would likely be sufficient. If, however, she sipped it slowly, James could pour another.

And because he had opened a brand new bottle right in front of her eyes, any suspicions she may have had would be eased.

But that was earlier, before they'd talked.

His brilliant plan.

That he no longer wanted to implement.

"Port comes in these tiny glasses, right?" said Brin, opening a cupboard and pulling down two crystal port glasses shaped like tulips. "I saw it in a movie once."

"Uh… right," nodded James. "I'll just… get the wine."

He walked around the corner into the pantry and through the door in the back to the small climate-controlled wine room. James had never been much of a drinker, but Carrie had often enjoyed a glass of wine with dinner.

He brought the port to the front of the room, one nearly empty, the other seemingly unopened. He held them both in his hands for a moment, feeling them light in one hand, heavy in the other. He set them on the tasting shelf near the door and stared down at them.

No. This was not the way.

He left the full, spiked bottle on the tasting shelf and brought the nearly empty bottle into the kitchen.

Brin had finished clearing and wiping the table. She sat in her chair again, with an empty port glass in front of her, another in front of James' seat.

"I'm sorry," James said. "It seems I only have enough port for one serving."

He pulled the stopper and filled Brin's glass, setting the empty bottle on the table before sitting across from her again.

Brin brought the glass to her lips. The deep ruby of the port set off the red of her hair and the pink of her lips, stirring something deep within James.

"That's alright," she said before taking a sip. "We can share."

17

WHATEVER BRIN HAD BEEN EXPECTING James to say by way of explanation for the extensive collection of women's clothing he had, she hadn't expected what she'd heard.

James was a little odd, a bit withdrawn and serious. Brin knew that already. But the man she saw tonight wasn't just odd or withdrawn. He was broken, his wounds seemingly as fresh today as they were years ago.

It broke Brin's heart to see it, and hers was a heart not easily broken.

Back downstairs in her bedroom, she sat on the edge of her bed and slipped off Carrie's dress, draping it neatly over a chair nearby, and changed back into the soft sweatpants and worn t-shirt James had given her.

Who could blame James for his brokenness? He'd suffered the cruelest fate. To have love stolen suddenly in its youth by disease and death was unnatural. Cruel. Unfair.

It explained why James had seemed so off when they were sharing the glass of port for dessert. He'd been even more with-drawn than usual. He would barely make eye contact with Brin. Once they'd emptied the glass, he'd taken it to the sink and immediately excused himself for bed.

Brin had handled it gracefully, of course. How could she not, after the painful story he'd shared. But, truth be told, Brin was disappointed. She'd felt a real connection forming between her and James during dinner. They'd talked and even laughed a bit. The food was delicious, the atmosphere quaint and endearing. And romantic.

And when he'd told her about his late fianceè, he'd shown such tenderness, such sensitivity, such depth of love for Carrie that Brin nearly fell in love with James right then and there. Brin was pretty sure none of her boyfriends had ever felt that way about her. She was damn sure she'd never felt that way about them.

As sad as the story was, Brin felt like James was happy to tell it, like it unburdened him somehow. There was an undercurrent of healing, of joy, even, while James spoke.

Or maybe Brin was projecting what she was feeling herself. Maybe James actually didn't feel anything toward Brin. Maybe he was just being nice, making a nice dinner for her, and she'd dredged up this horrible, painful past that he'd felt obligated to tell Brin about.

As much of a connection as Brin had felt, maybe James hadn't felt it at all. Maybe he'd just been drained by the conversation and had wanted to get rid of her as quickly as possible so he could be alone.

That would explain the sudden shift in his mood after she mentioned dessert.

Brin slipped under the covers and lay her head on her pillow, staring up at the beams crossing the ceiling. The covers felt heavy as she lay under them. Her head was a bit fuzzy, even from just one tiny glass of port.

She wasn't a big drinker, preferring to keep her wits about her most of the time. It had been a necessary policy during college, where the stream of drunken frat boys trying to get in her pants had been never-ending. She'd gotten in the habit of saying no and maintained it even after she graduated. When she and her friends went out, they would drink cosmos and dirty martinis and Brin would drink ice water.

So the port had hit her a bit harder than she'd expected. She wasn't drunk. Not even close. But she felt a warm furriness in her head that might have been pleasant if the evening had progressed the way she'd been hoping halfway through dinner.

As it turned out, the buzz was more of a nuisance than a pleasure. She lay looking at the ceiling, feeling dehydrated and clouded.

And frustrated.

She tossed and turned for a while, feeling hot and throwing the covers off, then feeling cold and pulling them back up, only to feel hot and throw them off again. All the while, her head felt fuzzier and her tongue felt thicker.

She pulled her sweatpants up to her knees and threw back the covers during another hot spell, but it didn't help. She was clammy, sweating. She felt like she was going to burst into flame at any moment. She finally just pulled off her sweatpants altogether and lay spread-eagled on the bed in just the t-shirt and her underwear.

For a brief, blissful second, a breeze came from somewhere and cooled her skin. But it passed as quickly as it had come. She began to overheat again. It felt like the air was close and stifling, like sleeping in a box of styrofoam peanuts. And her tongue felt like a box of cotton rounds stuffed in her mouth.

When she couldn't stand it anymore, when sleep finally stopped teasing and just abandoned her altogether, Brin sat up in bed with a huff and grabbed her crutches from the side of the bed. She clicked her way to the stairs and up to the kitchen for a glass of water.

The water felt so cool and cleansing on her tongue, Brin thought she might melt into a grateful puddle right there on the kitchen tile. She drained the first glass, filled it again and drained that, too. She filled it a third time and stood at the sink, catching her breath.

She ran cold water from the tap, filled her cupped hands with it, and held it against her face. Where she had been a thick, fuzzy, overheated mess before, she now felt herself returning to a state of clarity. Her overheated body cooled enough that her bare legs actually began to feel just a little bit chilly.

"Do you want me to turn up the air conditioning?" said James.

Brin jumped at the sound, nearly knocking over her water glass.

"Fuck," said Brin. She hadn't even heard his footsteps. "You're a sneaky one, aren't you?"

James' face darkened.

"What do you mean by that?"

Brin had been joking, but when she saw James' face, she felt nervous for a moment. Like she'd accidentally hit a nerve and made him... mad, or something. Brin couldn't imagine James being mad. He'd been nothing but kind. Even when he was in pain, he'd been kind.

"No, nothing," Brin said. "You scared me, that's all. I didn't hear you come in."

James nodded and came to the sink to open the cabinet and take out his own glass. He was dressed in a very light t-shirt and shorts, giving Brin a good view of his muscular arms and legs.

He had to reach past her to get the glass. When he did, their bare legs touched and Brin felt a sizzle of heat run up her spine and into her cheeks. Only this wasn't the fuzzy, stifling heat she'd felt before. This was a different kind of heat.

A much better kind.

James filled his glass with filtered water from the fridge. They stood there across from each other, each leaning against the sink, sipping cool water in silence.

"I thought you'd be asleep," said Brin.

James shrugged.

"Me, too," said Brin. "Tossing and turning. Couldn't get comfortable. Thought maybe a glass of water would help."

"And has it?" asked James.

His voice was husky and low. Brin suddenly felt her hot flash return.

"Not exactly," said Brin.

"Why is that?"

Brin felt suddenly aware that she was wearing only a t-shirt, and not a very long one, at that. The air against her bare skin felt electric. She knew that electricity wasn't because she felt cold.

She poured the rest of her water down the drain and set the glass in the sink, shifting her weight to rest on her one good leg, leaning against the sink. She turned to face James fully.

"I don't think water is what I really want," said Brin.

"No?" said James. He drained his own glass and set it in the sink beside Brin's. In doing so, he took a step closer to her.

Brin felt the electricity between them. James was close enough that she could feel the heat coming off of his body, through the thin t-shirt she wore. Every cell in her body, every impulse was pulling her toward James.

"What is it you really want?" asked James.

He was tall. She hadn't realized before how tall he was. Standing beside him, she tilted her chin up to see his eyes. In them, she saw hunger, passion.

Brin reached out to touch James' chest. She ley her hand over his heart, felt it beating quickly through the t-shirt. She ran her hand over his pectoral muscles, down to his abs. She felt them tight and defined. It was a surprise, one that sent a wave of intensity flooding through her body. She let her hand trace James' stomach, then around to his side and down to his hip.

He touched her cheek. His skin was soft and warm. His touch was gentle, but it ignited something in Brin. The heat that she'd been feeling suddenly became flame.

She tightened her hand on his side into a fist, grabbed a handful of his shirt, and pulled him toward her. With her other hand, she grabbed the back of his head and pulled his mouth down to hers.

She stumbled a bit as she did so, and James threw his arms around her to hold her. His arms were strong. They cradled her easily. She let herself melt back against them, thrust her chest and her hips forward, against his, pulled him down deeper into their kiss.

Brin had no doubt what she really wanted now.

18

James lay in bed in the dark and stared up at the ceiling.

Brin slept beside him. Her naked body was snuggled up to his, her head resting on his bare chest, her hair sprawled behind it. He felt her hair silky and cool against his skin, caressing and tickling with each breath he took.

Her arm was draped over his chest, a line of heat across his torso. Her leg was entwined with his.

Their lovemaking had been passionate, spontaneous.

Incredible.

He hadn't planned it.

Hadn't expected it.

Hadn't really even wanted it, especially after remembering what he had been planning with the port.

He couldn't even believe now he'd thought that to be a good idea only a few hours ago. It was despicable, to drug a woman senseless and transport them to another place and leave them there alone? Even if he were waiting, watching, making sure she was okay until the emergency vehicles arrived, how would Brin have felt waking up to that nightmare? Especially after the trauma she'd just been through.

And all for what? So that his precious hideout would stay hidden? Without even talking to Brin about keeping it secret?

No, James had been out of his mind.

It was a cruel and selfish plan and he hated himself for it now.

Especially now.

He'd succumbed to his baser impulses once more. He'd offended Carrie's memory by making love to Brin in the bed that was meant to be Carrie's. Even now, Brin lay in that bed, on the side that Carrie would have lain on.

And he'd offended that memory in another way.

Far worse.

"Mmmm," murmured Brin, shifting her position slightly. She snaked her arm farther across James' chest, pulled his naked body tighter against hers.

"You okay?" she whispered.

He felt her breasts against his side. Felt her pelvic bone against his hips as she squeezed his leg between hers.

She kissed his chest, her mouth warm and soft on his skin.

He felt something stir deep within himself.

Primal.

Wonderful.

Brin slid her hand down his chest.

Over his hips.

Between his legs.

"More than okay," she smiled.

Forgive me, Carrie.

James turned to his side and took Brin in his arms again.

19

The sex was unbelievable.

Brin lost all sense of time and space.

She'd even forgotten her injury for a while, though James was very careful, even in his passion, to make sure she was safe and well.

Oh, James had made sure Brin was very well, indeed.

The first time was pure passion, pure animal attraction.

The second time was like a happy, delirious confirmation that the first time had really happened.

But, the third time—Brin had never been with a man who was able to have a third time so quickly—was slow and tender, almost bittersweet.

At first.

From slow and tender, it built to soft and sensual.

Then to deep and passionate.

Then to aching and urgent.

Then to intense.

Then to absolutely fucking mindblowing.

Brin woke up who knows how much later from a blissfully exhausted sleep, sprawled on top of the covers, one leg draped over James' leg. Both of them had passed out, completely naked, completely spent.

Brin needed to pee, but she was honestly not sure if she could even walk.

And not because of the cast on her leg.

"Good morning," said James.

Brin turned her head. James was staring up at the ceiling.

"Not as good as last night," Brin said.

James turned his head to look at her, a faint smile on his face. He lifted one hand and stroked Brin's cheek softly with the back of it.

"I'll make breakfast," he said.

James stood from the bed and padded across the room, across their clothes scattered on the ground, to the bathroom on the far side of the hallway.

His bathroom.

I'll make breakfast? That's all he has to say?

Brin rolled up on one elbow and watched him walk.

It was a hell of a view.

It was always the nerdy, quiet ones. Why was it always them?

Well, sometimes it wasn't. Sometimes the nerdy quiet ones were soft and squishy and annoying all over.

But when they weren't...

And James wasn't.

There was nothing squishy on that body. And what was soft was only a temporary condition.

Brin could attest to that.

But, still. *I'll make breakfast*? That's all she got?

Brin flopped back down on her back on the bed and blew out a frustrated sigh. Then she closed her eyes and remembered last night. A smile crept across her face.

She'd sure as hell picked the right ridge to fall off of.

When Brin came into the kitchen and looked at the clock on the microwave, she couldn't believe how late it was. There were no windows in the bedroom. It was like being in a Vegas casino, where you lose all track of time amid the melodious beeps and chimes of the slot machines and the non-stop activity.

But it was already well after noon. The sliver of sunlight slanting through a small window at the top of the wall was soft and orange. The sun was already falling below the treeline.

They must have been at it well past dawn.

Brin had thrown on James' t-shirt that she'd picked up off the bedroom floor, but nothing else. No bra, no underwear, nothing.

Whatever that breakfast comment had meant earlier, she didn't want James to forget what had happened last night.

He was at the stove stirring something in a pot. Brin went to the espresso machine and started to pull shots. She did her best to agitate James. She bumped hips with him as she emptied the knock box in the trash. She stuck her bare ass out at him as she pulled the milk from the fridge. She reached up past him to grab two espresso glasses, intentionally reaching high enough to pull the t-shirt up past her hips, exposing her nakedness right in front of him.

He must have seen her. She was being comically obvious.

But he didn't say anything. Didn't even look away from the pot on the stove. He just stirred and stirred and smacked the wooden spoon against the pot, ignoring her completely.

That fucker.

Brin didn't know if she'd done something to upset James, but she honestly didn't care. She'd felt something last night, something more than just galaxy-class orgasms. She'd felt a real connection between herself and James.

The sex was just the result of that connection. She'd felt it building at the dinner table when they were eating. Then it intensified when James was talking about Carrie.

Then it got weird when they drank the port.

And then it exploded when they met each other at the sink later in the evening.

The sex was the result, not the starting point.

But, if James was in denial, if he was too scared to embrace it, if he was going to ghost Brin from two feet away, then fuck him.

Fuck him.

No man was worth that kind of bullshit, no matter how good the sex.

No matter how deep the connection.

Brin banged the portafilter from the espresso machine against the knock box a little harder than she meant to. Coffee grounds went everywhere. The sound of metal slamming against the box shook the tension-filled silence like a gunshot.

A gunshot.

The man with the dragon on his neck.

Holding a gun.

In the woods.

Firing it.

Brin running.

James whirled around, irritation on his face. Brin had lifted her arm to slam the portafilter down again, but she was lost in her memory.

James grabbed her wrist in the air before she could bring it down again. The irritation on his face melted into concern when his eyes met Brin's.

"Brin?" he said, his voice soft and deep.

Brin just stared back at him, at his deep brown eyes.

Brown beard.

Bald head.

The gunshot.

The man holding the gun.

Dragon.

Brin running.

Gunshot.

"Brin?" said James again. He dropped her wrist and put a hand on each of her shoulders, squaring Brin's face to look directly into his.

"Brin, what is it?"

Did he see her?

Had the bald man with the brown beard and the dragon tattoo on his neck seen Brin after he murdered someone with his gun?

"Brin," said James, a note of panic slipping into his voice. "What's wrong?"

Brin stared at James. She felt like he was in another world, another time. Like he was behind glass.

"I remember," she whispered.

20

When he woke next to Brin, she looked so beautiful in the soft light from the lamp they'd left on all night.

Or all morning. James had lost track of time.

He'd lost track of everything. Including himself.

Including the world around him.

It had all exploded, leaving only Brin, only her body and his body.

Her heart and his heart.

She looked so beautiful that James immediately felt guilty for even being there. For even being with her.

She was his patient, someone who had come before him in need of help. And now he'd gone and slept with her.

Two days after dragging her unconscious body into his home.

The home he'd built for his dead fianceè.

Right after he'd intended to drug Brin to drag her down the mountain.

It was all just too damn creepy, too evil for him to even think about. He was disgusted with himself, with his own depravity.

Brin was incredible. He'd felt that instinctively when he first saw her on the video feed, but he knew it for sure now.

She deserved someone far better than him.

He knew she was hurt, confused when he left the bedroom so abruptly. That was probably for the best. It was best for her if she just forgot about James.

And if she couldn't forget about him, it was best if she hated him. That would be better for Brin than the alternative.

If she knew the truth, she would hate him anyway.

If he had to, James would tell her. If that's what he needed to do to drive her away for good, so be it.

He needed to get her back to civilization more than ever now, but not to protect his precious fucking isolation. He still couldn't believe how callous and petty and selfish his intentions had been.

No, now he needed to get her to civilization just to get her away from him. For her own sake.

James could wallow in self-hatred alone. He'd been getting quite good at that over the last few years. It was what he deserved. He saw that now. Fate had a way of giving us what we deserve. Cosmic justice, James supposed.

And James deserved to die alone.

Brin did not.

Brin deserved someone as incredible as she was.

So, James had left the bedroom abruptly, coldly.

He made plain oatmeal for breakfast. Gloopy, bland plain oatmeal. The most unattractive, boring, off-putting meal he could think of.

It was stupid, he knew, but he was doing whatever he could think of to put Brin off.

And then she'd come into the kitchen wearing nothing but his t-shirt.

And it was an old t-shirt, too.

Practically see-through.

And he tried not to see through it, tried not to look. But, goddamn. An unmarried man can only do so much when a gorgeous naked woman is bumping his hip and pressing her ass into him and rubbing her naked pelvis against him.

His body was reacting. It was straining for release just as much as he was straining to contain it. James wanted nothing more than to take Brin right there, with a sweep of his arm send the plates and glasses shattering off the table and have Brin herself for breakfast.

But, he bit down hard on his cheeks, hard enough that he tasted blood in his mouth. He focused on the oatmeal, that goddamn tasteless oatmeal, stirring and stirring and pounding the sticky, gloopy shit off the wooden spoon again and again.

Then, Brin was pounding something behind him, something loud, and wet, dark brown clumps of ground coffee flew into the oatmeal.

James snapped.

He spun around, all control lost. He didn't know if he was angry or aching. Brin's arm was in the air. James didn't know why. Didn't stop to think. He just grabbed her wrist.

He found her lips, hungry for them, found her eyes, drinking them in like a man who's been crawling through the desert and found water at last.

But something broke through his hunger, his thirst.

Something in her eyes.

Something wrong.

She had wet chunks of coffee grounds all over her t-shirt, her cheeks, in her hair.

Her eyes were wide open, vacant and terrified all at once.

Fear suddenly stabbed through James.

He called her. She didn't respond. That faraway, frightened look stayed in her eyes.

The fear grew in James.

Finally, she whispered, "I remember."

"You remember?" James replied. "What do you remember?

"I remember," Brin said again, mumbling. The faraway look

left her eyes as she seemed to come back into an awareness of her surroundings. She looked at James with clarity and focus.

Then she grabbed her crutches and walked away.

James followed her as she clicked and swung down the hallway. Occasionally, she would stop and stare into space or stare at a wall, muttering to herself.

"What is it, Brin?" he pleaded. "What do you remember?"

It must be her memories from before her fall. What else could it be?

An wave of fear passed over James, an irrational fear that she had somehow figured out what he had been planning to do before last night.

But, he knew that was impossible.

Brin clicked and swung and muttered past the machine room, through the office and the library, back again to the kitchen, James following all the way. She stared at the refrigerator for a moment, then suddenly, dropped into a chair by the table.

James sat down opposite her, trying to make eye contact. Trying to understand what was happening, what she was thinking.

Finally, she looked up at James.

Her eyes were hard and serious.

Again, a wave of irrational fear swept through James.

"What is it, Brin?" he whispered.

"James," she replied. "I think we may be in trouble."

21

It all came flooding back to Brin.

Getting lost on the way down from the peak, going off the gravel road into the woods when she heard voices, then hoping to get directions from the man in the clearing.

The bald man with the beard and the tattoo on his neck who was pointing a gun at someone Brin could not see, someone who was pleading. Pleading for his life.

It was a man's voice she had heard pleading.

Then the gunshot.

Then running wildly through the woods until she fell.

Brin told James everything.

He sat in stunned silence for a long moment. He didn't seem upset or angry or frightened. He just seemed... shocked.

"Did the man see you?" he finally asked.

Not shocked, it turns out. Just processing the information, turning it over and over. The man's mind was incredible. Like a computer.

"Not that I saw," Brin answered, "but I was running away as soon as I heard the shot. Maybe even before I heard it."

James nodded.

"And nothing showed up on the camera footage," he said, "when I scanned it to try to see what you'd been running from."

"So either he didn't see me at all," Brin mused, "or he saw me and didn't follow, or he tried to follow and I lost him in the woods."

James nodded.

"Right," he said. "And all of that was... what... three days ago now?"

He ran his hand through his tousled bedhead. The movement was so impossibly cute, Brin nearly forgot all about the killer who might be looking for her.

"I'm losing track," said Brin.

She smiled. James smiled back.

Brin shook herself from the fantasies suddenly racing through her mind.

Focus. Killer on the loose.

Plus, five minutes ago, James was cold-shouldering her. Brin hadn't forgotten about that.

She pulled the smile off her face and fixed James with a hard stare. To her satisfaction, his face went white and he sat back in his chair like she'd slapped him.

"We've got to get out of here," she said. "We can't let that guy find us."

James gulped hard, then seemed to try to refocus his mind on the problem at hand.

"Right," he said. "Well, we don't know for sure that he's even looking for you. And he's unlikely to be looking for me. If one of us needs to go outside, I'm probably safer than you would be."

Figures.

But, James had a point.

"He didn't see my face," she said. "I'm pretty sure of that. If he saw anything memorable, it was probably my red jacket."

That Patagonia jacket was bright red, like a fire engine. It was a bold, vibrant color that always lifted Brin's spirits. But, now, it might get her killed.

"So you can't wear that jacket, then," said James.

He looked up at her and pursed his lips.

"What?" said Brin. "It's okay. I can go without a jacket."

"Not that," said James. "He might have seen your hair, too. It's pretty unique."

Shit. He was right. Her hair was nearly as bright as her jacket.

"You can cut it," said James. "Or dye it a different color."

"Oh, yeah?" Brin retorted. "You got a hair salon down there by the fucking MRI machine?"

"Well... no," said James. "But I do have scissors."

"How about a hat, James. You got one of those?"

Fucking men. Just cut your hair with some dull scissors or dump a bucket of black paint on it. That'll fix everything.

Idiots.

Though if she got herself killed because she didn't want to ruin her hair, Brin would be the idiot then.

She didn't think it would come to that. She'd stay inside. She couldn't get around very well outside, anyway, with a cast and crutches. And if she needed to go out she would wear a hat.

"Yes," nodded James quickly. Very quickly. "I have a hat. I have lots of hats."

Brin smiled to herself. He was already backpedaling from his cold behavior earlier. That was good.

She'd make him sweat a bit longer, though. Teach him to treat a woman with some fucking respect.

"Okay, fine," Brin said. "So I'll stay inside, wear a hat, don't wear my jacket." She rapped her knuckles on the table and chewed her lip, thinking. "In the meantime, how do we figure out if this guy is out there looking for me?"

James smiled at that. He looked awfully smug. Brin just raised an eyebrow.

James pointed to the array of flat screen TVs on the wall behind Brin. They were covered in boxes showing live video feeds from various vantage points around the forest and inside the house.

"Leave that part to me," he said.

22

James surveyed the equipment in his parts room, looking for as many working cameras and monitors as he could find. So far, he counted fifteen monitors and thirty-seven cameras, of which twenty-nine were operational. The others had fallen victim to the elements or a fallen tree branch or a curious and destructive woodland creature.

James needed to beef up his visual survey of the area. If this killer was out there looking for Brin, James wanted to know about it.

And he wanted to know as soon as possible.

The current surveillance perimeter was ample, but it was designed to give James plenty of notice—and some options for deterrence—if an intruder looked like they might stumble upon his home.

It was a defensive perimeter.

Right now, they needed an offensive perimeter.

James needed to be actively looking throughout the area to determine if this killer was on the hunt. To do that, he needed more cameras, covering a much wider area. That meant not just more hardware, but a more robust signaling network, as well.

It was impractical to use wired hardware in a forest environment. Even setting aside the difficulty of obtaining, installing, and maintaining the miles of cable that would be needed, wired hardware was more susceptible to damage and less flexible in terms of positioning than their wireless counterparts.

Wireless components gave the advantage of flexiblity, ease of setup, and relatively low maintenance. But they came with the disadvantage of slower speed and shorter communication distance. Instead of wires carrying information at high speed, the wireless devices needed to talk to each other or to some kind of base station in order to relay information back to the central system.

With some foresight, James could have set up a cellular system or even a satellite system. But the original purpose for the surveillance system had lent itself very well to a wireless system over a relatively small area.

Now, he would have to work with those limitations to try as best he could to bend that network to a purpose it was not designed to fulfill.

Cameras, wireless repeaters, more monitors to allow for more camera feeds. And a beefed up facial recognition algorithm to look for a bald man with a scruffy beard and a tattoo on his neck.

And if James couldn't pull it together, couldn't find the hardware in his storage and make it work, this man might find them.

Might find Brin.

And if he did, he would kill her.

She was a witness to a murder the man had committed in cold blood. And from Brin's brief description, James had a feeling it wasn't the man's first kill.

James gathered the working cameras into a shoulder bag slung over his shoulder. He grabbed four monitors, two under each arm, and dropped them off under existing monitor arrays throughout the house. James would mount them when he had a chance, but he could at least wire them up to display the feeds from the new cameras.

Which meant he would need more wiring inside the house to accommodate the new monitors.

Fortunately, he had built in plenty of excess capacity when he'd built the house. He'd run twice as much wire to every port as he felt he needed. Technology has a tendency to proliferate, at least until it becomes burdensome and a breakthrough allows for the old tech to be cleaned out and the new tech installed, so it can proliferate anew.

He just needed to light up a few circuits, make sure everything was properly connected, and hook up the new monitors.

He went downstairs and unlocked the door to the telecom room. As he did so, he glanced over his shoulder into Brin's room.

Brin's room.

He'd started thinking of the sickbay that way. It had only been two days? Three days since Brin had arrived? And already James had her moving in.

Brin was sitting in the chair by her bed, messing with her cast. She looked up and saw him.

"What're you doing over there?" she asked.

"What're you doing?" James replied.

"I asked you first."

"True," James said, "but I'm not tearing apart a necessary medical device that's helping me heal."

"Neither am I," Brin said, indignant. "I'm just scratching under my cast. It itches like hell and it's driving me fucking crazy."

"Well, try not to scratch too hard." James pointed to a pile of fiberglass and casting tape forming at Brin's feet. "There won't be much cast left at the rate you're going."

Brin waved him off.

James turned back to the door and pushed it open.

"I've been wondering what's in there for days," said Brin.

"Just a bunch of wiring," James said. "It's the telecom room, where all the wiring for the house comes together. CAT-5, AV, even the electrical all flows through this room. Makes it easier to maintain and expand." He gestured to the open door. "Come take a tour, if you want."

"I'm good," said Brin, giving her leg one last hard scratch before flopping back in her chair, clearly unsatisfied. "These crutches are giving me pit sores. I'm just gonna lay off them for a bit." She eyed the bed. "Maybe I'll take a nap."

James couldn't believe she could even think about taking a nap knowing that a killer might be out there looking for her. He watched her hop on her good foot over to the bed, flop down, and cover her eyes with her arm.

He moved over and flicked the light switch, turning off the lights in Brin's room.

"Thanks," she mumbled from behind her arm.

James watched her lay there. Beautiful, intelligent, fiery.

And still injured.

He needed to do something about that, too.

And he had an idea that just might work.

23

BRIN WAS surprised she fell asleep so quickly. Hell, she was surprised she fell asleep at all. But, she'd been so tired after her long night-morning with James, then the tension over breakfast, then the memories and planning that followed. She fell asleep almost as soon as her head touched her pillow.

And stayed asleep for a long time.

When Brin woke, she was disoriented, unsure of what time of day it was or even where she was for a moment. Her mouth tasted stale and dry and her stomach was making alarming gurgling noises.

She was starved.

Once her head started to clear, she worked her way upstairs. She was developing a technique with one hand on the railing, the other on the crutches, and something halfway between a hop and a tricep press to get up each stair. With the number of times she'd gone up and down in the last few days, she was getting to be fairly fast.

Okay, maybe "fast" was too generous a word, but she was definitely faster than she'd been when she started.

She made her way to the kitchen. It was empty, but she could smell something cooking. The stove had nothing on it, so she took a quick peek in the oven and saw some kind of chicken with roasting vegetables. The smell of the savory chicken and the seasoned vegetables—red onion and mushrooms and fennel—made Brin's mouth water and her stomach growl again in a very demanding way.

James had started dinner.

That meant Brin must have slept for at least three or four hours.

Brin wandered the halls. James wasn't in the library or his office. When she came through into the machine room, she found him there, pulling what looked like a pair of curved sticks out of one of the smaller machines. In the center of each stick was a donut-shaped connector. The sticks were joined in the center. Altogether, it looked like a weird, curvy letter 'H' with the donuts on either side of the crossbar.

"What's that?" said Brin.

James spun, startled.

"Sorry," said Brin. "Didn't mean to sneak up on you."

"You were asleep for a long time," James said. "Dinner's in the oven."

"Yeah, I saw that. Smells good."

James nodded and stared down at the H-shaped object in his hand.

Silence fell like a bag of bricks.

Why was this all so awkward? Last night had been incredible. Brin was pretty sure James had felt the same. Then this morning he'd been an asshole. And now he was tiptoing around her, walking on eggshells, acting all weird again.

Honestly, if he was this moody all the time, to hell with him. Brin had more important things to do with her life than babysit yet another man-child.

And yet...

"What's that?" asked Brin, nodding toward the object in James' hand.

"Just an idea I'm working on," he said. He seemed almost shy about it. "It's not ready yet."

Despite her irritation, Brin couldn't help thinking it was cute the way James was protective of his idea, unwilling to show it to Brin or talk about it before it was done. Brin sometimes felt that way about a painting or a sculpture when it was brand new.

They were always so fragile in the beginning, before they built up enough weight to stand on their own. Before then, when they were more idea than object, it was too easy to shatter them into a million pieces. An unkind word or a critical thought or even just a bad day could send that idea blowing away in the wind.

But, if you sheltered it, nurtured it, build it for a while until it accumulated enough gravity in itself, then it could withstand the unkindnesses and criticisms a bit better. Once it got a toehold on reality, it could withstand the abuse a bit better.

Easier said than done.

"Any progress on finding that guy?" asked Brin.

"No, not yet," James said. "I haven't seen any sign of him on the monitors."

James turned and set the object on a shelf beside a bunch of other parts, including the one shaped like a leg that Brin had seen the other day.

"But," James continued, "I found a bunch of spare cameras in the parts room. I beefed up the network to accommodate them, so tomorrow I'll set them out in the woods and widen our surveillance perimeter."

Brin nodded.

The awkward silence returned.

It was really annoying.

Well, if James was going to be immature about it, that didn't mean Brin had to be. She was stuck in this house in the middle of the woods with a broken leg and no means of communication with the outside world. On top of that, there was a killer who might be looking for her.

And she was dependent on a moody weirdo for her health and protection.

Brin needed to get some control of this situation. Fast.

"Look, James," she said, as kindly as she could, "I don't know why everything suddenly feels so awkward here."

James flushed red and immediately turned his back to her, pretending to work with the objects on the shelf, but Brin could see he was just rearranging them.

Another man-child.

Brin sighed.

"Last night was great," Brin continued. "Amazing, really."

It truly had been incredible. Brin was still a little surprised by that fact.

And the memory of it got her body tingling in all sorts of delightfully uncomfortable ways.

She pushed those sensations out of her mind.

"But it was just a thing, James. We had an amazing night. Doesn't mean we have to get married or anything. We're both consenting adults here, right?"

James turned and looked at her. The awkwardness was gone. He wasn't avoiding eye contact with her anymore.

Good. Maybe he feels better. Maybe he just wanted to be let off the hook.

Brin felt a little hurt at that thought, but it was better than the weirdness that had fallen between them.

James started to say something, opened his mouth to speak, but shut it again. Then just stared at Brin, thoughtfully.

"Penny for your thoughts?" she said.

Again, he opened his mouth to speak. Again, he seemed to reconsider and shut it.

He looked like a fucking goldfish.

"For fuck's sake, James, just spit it out."

James nodded and gave a thin smile.

A long beep sounded from down the hallway in the kitchen.

"I'd better go check on dinner," he said, and left the room.

24

James had almost come out and said it.

He wanted to.

But, he knew how pathetic it would sound.

Brin, I think I love you, but I hardly know you. And it doesn't matter anyway because you deserve way better than a shit like me.

It would sound pathetic and, worse, James was afraid Brin would agree. That she would laugh in his face.

She'd already said that last night was just a fling. Didn't mean anything to her.

That hurt, James had to admit. It was for the best, but it hurt to think that the experience that had been so earth-shattering for James was just another one-night stand for Brin.

But, it was for the best.

James was not a good man right now. He was cheating on the memory of his dead fianceè with a girl he'd been planning to drug into catatonia and leave stranded alone in the woods.

Not much to hold his head up about.

He was not good enough for Brin, and she seemed to agree.

But, he could still do whatever was in his power to get her home safely. He was determined to do at least that much.

Dinner now. Cameras tomorrow.

And between, his little gadget would probably be ready.

They ate dinner mostly in silence. It wasn't hostile, just awkward. James' mind was a non-stop recording of self-recrimination.

You're betraying Carrie.

You're a date-rape drugger.

You're a selfish prick who cares more about being alone than about the safety of an innocent woman.

And every time he looked up at Brin, she looked so beautiful in the soft overhead lighting. Desire rose in James. Memories of last night came to his mind.

And then the self-recrimination would come back twice as loud.

It was painful to endure, so much so that James just avoided eye contact with Brin as much as possible. At least that way, he only had to deal with the self-recrimination and not the added pain of the desire, the memories, and the impossibility of them ever happening again.

Brin offered to clean up, but James insisted on doing it himself, so Brin excused herself and went downstairs for the evening, leaving James alone for the night.

He knew of only one way to endure the cycle of pain caused by his own thoughts. He'd figured it out after Carrie died, when he had moved into this house all alone. It was the only thing that kept him sane, that kept him from slitting his own wrists.

He worked.

Those first few months, he'd worked until he passed out from exhaustion at his desk. When he woke up a few hours later, the thoughts would quickly return, so he would work again, pushing himself longer hours.

He wasn't eating, was sleeping only an hour or two each day. He lost weight. A lot of it. His mouth began to taste like a dead rat and his body started to smell like one. Personal hygiene was not a priority.

The days blurred into each other and he fell into a kind of working delirium. In retrospect, he had been suffering from extreme sleep deprivation and probably low blood sugar, but at the time, the delirium was a godsend, for it finally put an end to the loop of self-hatred that had been playing in his mind for months.

It also pushed him to a breakthrough in his work.

He'd been dabbling in robotics ever since he'd sold his first company to Google for three hundred million dollars. "Company" was a grandiose term, though it was legally accurate. James' "company" was just him and the search algorithm he'd written, which he was licensing to companies across Silicon Valley for princely sums.

They called it the "Google killer", so it was only a matter of time before Google approached him. They'd courted him for months, throwing more and more money his way. Their one stipulation was that he come to work for them for a few years. But James flatly refused, again and again. He'd give up his algorithm, but he would not give up his freedom.

They eventually capitulated, as he figured they would. Three hundred million dollars is pocket change to a company like Google, and James knew the algorithm he'd created was valuable to them.

Since then, he'd pursued an interest not just in data science and software development, which were his core skills, but in their application to physical objects. Robotics, nanotech, even the buzzy bullshit called "the internet of things" were interesting extensions of his skills.

He'd been deep into the topic when he met Carrie. When she got sick, his efforts naturally turned toward medical applications, especially nanobiotechnology. He had been focused on building a microscopic biosensor that could detect cancer at the cellular level and leave a marker on the cancerous cells. Another bit of nanotech could then be deployed to destroy those cells. It was like an artificial immune system.

But it didn't work.

At least, not well enough or fast enough to save Carrie.

But after she died, when he was on the brink of insanity and suicide, James had poured himself back into the work. Months became years and with the work as his lifeline, James slowly crawled out of his depression.

He thought he may have finally solved the problems he'd had in earlier iterations and was about to run his test suite again to verify it when Brin had come crashing into his life.

And now, he was moving from the nano scale to the human scale again, going back to his early robotics explorations to make a device that would enable Brin to move freely under her own power, without crutches, even on unstable terrain like the soft, steep slopes of the mountain outside.

In fact, James had already started building the device, though he didn't know it at the time. When Brin first came in and James realized her leg was broken, his first instinct was to fabricate a carbon-fiber cast for her. Then he realized that without precise measurements the fit would be too rough and would likely cause more harm than good. It would rub against her skin in places and allow too much loose movement elsewhere, likely leading to sores and ulcers. There were workarounds, of course, but James finally realized they were too time-consuming and troublesome for the problem at hand. He reverted to using standard casting materials and techniques.

But, he still had the plans for the carbon-fiber cast. With a little tweaking and a few more parts, he repurposed it to this new application.

And the device was coming together quickly. He'd never built anything like it before, but the design and application was so obvious to him now that he couldn't believe he hadn't thought of it right off the bat. It was so much simpler—and more ethical—than his ridiculous plan to drug Brin and drag her out of the forest in the middle of the night. He'd just been too focused on that plan—on his own fears, really—to step back and look for a more creative solution.

Nonetheless, James had woken up that morning, after his incredible night with Brin, and the idea for this device just popped into his head, fully formed. An exoskeleton, one that covered Brin's cast, with supports and a sensor array running over her knee and halfway up her thigh for stability and better data on the orientation of her leg. A gyroscope and accelerometer embedded in the device would work in concert with the ones in Brin's cell phone to monitor the position of her broken leg in relation to the rest of her body. Tiny motors in the foot and in the knee would then react to self-correct her balance, as well as provide an amplification of her muscle power whenever she pushed off with her foot.

If it worked—and James was quite sure it would—Brin's bad leg would be stronger than her good leg.

He was building it from materials he had at home, building it on his CNC machines and 3-D printers. They were very good machines, but the result would not be perfect. It would not be the same as a precision milled device produced in a medical-grade manufacturing facility. It wasn't going to be a true exoskeleton that could be used clinically in the real world.

But it would be enough to get Brin down the mountain safely.

James went to the machine room, gathered up the parts he'd finished building earlier, and took them into his office for assembly. He'd be up all night, but he would get it done.

He would do it for Brin.

25

BRIN LAY in bed staring at the ceiling for hours.

She'd switched off the monitors showing the camera surveillance. The room was dark and cool.

Still, sleep wasn't going to come easy. She knew it. She could feel it. But she refused to get up and go upstairs.

She could hear James moving around up there and she didn't want to run into him again.

Though when she'd run into him the previous night, it had led to one of the best nights of her life.

Followed by one of the worst days.

Brin had just dumped one asshole. She sure as hell wasn't going to pine after another one. No matter how good the sex was.

But something about it just wouldn't let her go, wouldn't let her push it from her mind.

The sex had been incredible, but it was more than that.

There was something about James. A quiet kindness. An intelligent compassion. Something different from any man Brin had known.

Something she desperately craved.

Something she felt she needed.

Something that could help her get out of the drifting current she was in and push toward shore.

She heard a banging noise from upstairs, like James was hanging a picture or something, banging a hammer against the wall. What the hell was he doing up there?

No. Brin was not going to go up and look.

Aside from his kindness and compassion, there was also something deeply sad about James. He tried to hide it, Brin thought, but she could feel it anyway. Probably something about his fianceè, some sense of guilt. Survivor's guilt, maybe.

Whatever the cause, it seemed so tragic in such a helpful and talented person. She wanted to help him through it, like he'd been helping her get through her injuries. Return the favor.

Maybe if she could get him to open up about it, to admit the deep, dark secrets that were weighing on him, he could heal and move on. He'd opened up about Carrie. Maybe Brin could get him to open up about this, too.

As she mulled this possibility, Brin felt sleep finally start to overtake her. The noises from upstairs continued, now a drilling noise. But it was a soft, soothing sound in the back of her mind now.

She fell asleep to it, thinking of James.

When Brin woke, she could still hear the drilling sound.

At first she thought she was dreaming. But after she rubbed her eyes, swung her legs over the side of the bed, and sat up, she heard the sound again.

Had she only slept for a few minutes? A power nap?

No, Brin had never been a napper. Whenever she tried to take a ten-minute power nap, she'd wake up an hour and a half later, cranky as all hell.

And right now she felt great, like she'd had a full night's

sleep.

She switched the surveillance monitors on again and saw images of bright morning sunshine.

Had James worked through the night?

What the hell for?

Brin collected her crutches and hopped upstairs, stopping first in the bathroom to pee and to wash her face. Then to the kitchen for a hot cup of espresso. The coffee tasted fantastic, rich and complex on her tongue. She was starting to feel like herself again, minus the cast slowing her down.

She heard James again, moving around in the machine room down the hall, and pulled an espresso shot for him, too, dumping it into a travel mug with a lid so she could bring it to him on her crutches without spilling everything on the way.

When she got to the room, James had his back toward her, hunched over something laid out on the table at the back of the room.

"Good morning," Brin said. "I brought you come coffee."

She held out the cup to him as he turned around.

He looked like hell.

His hair was a mess and he was wearing the same clothes he'd had on the night before at dinner. His eyes were sunken, with dark bags underneath, and his face was ashen, his full stubble the only color on it. He looked like an addict who hadn't had his fix in a while.

"Thanks," he said, taking the coffee, draining it in one swig, and handing the cup back to Brin.

Seemed a little presumptuous to Brin. She was being nice, bringing him some coffee, and now James thought she was his serving wench?

She took the cup from James and set it on a shelf beside her. Brin sniffed the air. It smelled like a mix of man sweat and morning breath. She moved back a step into the doorway to collect a little fresher air from the hallway.

"What are you working on?" she asked.

"It's almost done," James said, breathless and distracted.

He leaned down with a tiny screwdriver and adjusted something, then tapped on a laptop beside him. There were wires running from the laptop to whatever was on the table, hidden by James body.

"Have you been up all night working on this?" Brin asked.

"What?" said James without turning.

"I said, did you get any sleep last night, James?"

"What?" he said again, his voice the distracted, half-hollow sound of someone whose voice was making noises without input from his brain.

Brin shook her head. He wasn't even listening to her.

"It's almost done," James murmured, tapping a few more times on the laptop.

"Good for you, James," said Brin, turning to leave the room. "I'm just gonna go get some breakfast."

"Yes!" shouted James, holding his hands out in front of him, staring at the computer screen. It beeped and flashed green. "Yes!" James shouted again. "It works!"

Brin heard a heavy thud behind her. She stopped and turned back to see James, his face jubilant, holding the top of what looked like a black plastic leg in a cage. The heavy thud must have come when James dropped the contraption down onto the floor.

It was like the old leg braces they used in the fifties, with the metal bars running up the side of the legs, fastened across the front with more metal bars.

Only the contraption in front of James was black plastic and only seemed to be half of a leg.

"It works?" asked Brin.

James nodded eagerly.

"That's great, James." He definitely didn't sleep last night, because he was acting like a loon. "What does it do?"

"What does it do?" he said, like he couldn't believe Brin didn't already know. He honestly seemed confused by the question.

"Yes, James," Brin said. "What the hell is it?"

She sounded exasperated, and she was. But she was also mildly amused by this man standing before her, exhausted and energized, like a little kid who'd just spent hours building his first complex Lego piece all by himself.

"It's an exoskeleton," James said.

"Oh really?"

Brin understood the term from her science classes. It was something related to insects. But she didn't understand why James was using it in reference to the thing standing between them.

"Well, only a partial exoskeleton, but, still..."

He didn't say anything else after that. Just looked at Brin with a silly grin on his face.

A silly, charming, childlike grin.

Brin couldn't help but laugh.

"Okay, great. Good job, James. You built an exoskeleton. Well," she corrected herself, "a partial one, at least." She turned to head down the hallway. "Now, I'm going to fix myself some breakfast." She looked over her shoulder at James. "You look like you could use some, too. And maybe a nap."

She started down the hallway when she felt James' hand on her shoulder. His grip was gentle, but firm. Like the other night, it sent electric shockwaves coursing through Brin's body, stirring up all sorts of thoughts and feelings she was trying desperately to ignore.

"Brin," said James, his deep voice soft and close in her ear.

An involuntary shiver of pleasure ran down Brin's spine. She turned her head and looked into James' deep, clear brown eyes.

"I made it for you," he said.

26

JAMES WANTED to fit Brin with the exoskeleton right away, but she insisted that he have some breakfast first. James was so keyed up from lack of sleep and the thrill of finishing that he didn't think he'd be able to eat. His stomach was a hard, shriveled walnut. It had been fifteen hours since he'd last eaten or drunk. He didn't want the distraction of physical sustenance. He was riding the high of a complex problem finally solved.

That is, until the first forkful of French toast hit his tongue. Then he scarfed up every bite on his plate and asked for more. Brin was still at the stove cooking her own serving when James was finished with his. She just laughed and dished her toast onto his plate and made more for herself.

James went to pull an espresso shot, but Brin smacked him on the back of his hand with the spatula. She swung hard. It stung like a rubber band snapping against James' skin.

"No more coffee," said Brin. "You need to get some sleep or you'll be fucking useless today."

James was initially offended, his pride hurt, but it quickly faded. He grinned at Brin.

"I don't need coffee, anyway," he said. It didn't matter that he hadn't slept in over twenty-four hours. The adrenaline was coursing through his veins. He'd felt this way many times in the past, always on the heels of some breakthrough or another, some thorny problem cleared away, some Gordian knot sliced clean through.

While Brin ate her own breakfast, James carried the exoskeleton into the kitchen and kneeled beside her to prep it for her fitting. He had tweaked the design to hollow out what was originally meant to be her leg cast. It was much thinner and lighter now, and was sliced longitudinally so that James could fit it easily around Brin's existing leg cast. Two cross-bands would hold it together.

Several times, as James was prepping the unit, he tried to line it up with Brin's leg, tried to start fitting it. He would lean it up against her leg where it was slanted under the table or try to pull her leg out to line things up. Brin would slap his hand away every time and stubbornly pull her leg back under the table, swearing at him more and more forcefully every time.

James knew he was being a pest, but he was too excited to stop. He wished Brin would eat faster.

It seemed to James that she was intentionally eating slower just to frustrate him. When she got up to pull herself a second shot of espresso, then sat back down to sip it slowly, he was sure of it.

At last, she turned in her chair, swinging her legs from under the table.

"All right, James," she said, a slight smile on her lips. "What the fuck am I supposed to do with this thing?"

The moment was finally here. James had been waiting for what seemed like a lifetime. But in that moment, a calm descended over him.

He wasn't going to rush it.

He was going to do it right.

Brin needed to understand this thing that was going to be strapped to her body. It wasn't a toy and could potentially cause injury if it was misused, especially if it torqued in the wrong direction and exacerbated the leg fracture.

"This is an exoskeleton," began James.

"A partial exoskeleton," Brin said.

James looked up at her.

She was smiling.

He smiled back.

"Right," he replied. "A partial exoskeleton."

"And it goes on my leg?"

She moved her foot forward on her uninjured leg.

"Yes, it goes on your leg," James said, "but not that one."

"It goes on… the broken leg?"

"Exactly. It'll provide support for that leg. Much more support than just the cast."

Brin tucked her bad leg under her chair away from James, a dubious look on her face.

"You're not taking my cast off," she said. "I don't want to deal with all of that shit right now."

"No," James said, "we don't need to remove your cast. The exoskeleton will fit over the top of it."

Brin thought for a moment, then nodded and slowly held out her casted leg.

"Alright," she said. "Let's give it a shot."

James lined up the two halves of the exoskeletal casting with the sides of Brin's leg cast. They fit well, but not well enough for a snug fit. In the absence of a more precise casting, James needed something to fill in the small variances between the casting and Brin's leg.

"Be right back," he said.

He ran back to the machine room and pulled a block of soft foam from the supply cabinet. He quickly used a hacksaw to cut off two pieces of roughly the right size and dashed back to the kitchen with them.

Brin was examining the exoskeletal harness, peering closely at the servos in the knee joints.

"Is this some kind of robotic thing?" she asked.

"Sort of," replied James as he stuffed a sheet of foam on the inside of one half of the exoskeletal casting and pressed it against Brin's leg. The foam compressed easily and created a snug fit between the two surfaces.

"You gonna make me into some kind of bionic woman?"

James did the same with the other half and secured them to Brin's leg with the two cross-braces, tightening them with a screwdriver until he was sure they wouldn't slip.

"The bionic woman had bio-implants," he said, "and an endoskeleton, I think." He took the harness from Brin and slotted it into the top of the casting. "This is an exoskeleton, remember?"

"Well," said Brin, "just a partial exoskeleton."

James was pretty sure that joke was going to stick around for a while.

He tightened the harness to the casting and fitted the cross-brace loosely around Brin's thigh. He'd lined the upper braces with foam where they contacted Brin's leg to prevent chafing. Without that, it could bruise Brin or even tear skin off her leg under the wrong circumstances.

He checked the screws again to make sure they were all tight, then snapped in the wires that connected the lower sensors to the upper sensors. The two parts were hardwired to each other for speed of communication, but the whole exoskeleton would communicate with Brin's smartphone wirelessly. Not the fastest, but should be fast enough for most conditions. The differences in speed were on the order of nanoseconds.

James ran into the machine room to grab his laptop, then ran the same diagnostics he'd run earlier to make sure everything was still working properly. When his computer beeped and all the checks on his screen were flashing green, he blew out a sigh.

This was it.

"Ready?" he asked, looking up at Brin from his knees.

"Since I still don't know what this thing really does, I'll just go ahead and say 'sure'."

"Okay," James said. "Stand up."

Brin moved to stand.

"Wait!" said James.

Brin froze.

"Sorry," he said. "Forgot one thing. Did you bring your phone?"

Brin had turned off her phone and left it by her bed since James had lied and told her it had no connection. She'd seemed surprised when he said he needed it for this, but she'd brought it up for him.

He powered it on.

"Your battery is only at five percent," he said. He sounded incredulous, like he couldn't believe anyone would let their battery run out. He looked at her like he was waiting for an apology or an explanation.

Brin just shrugged.

"What's your passcode?" James asked, shaking his head.

Brin looked askance at James for a moment, then held out her hand. James rolled his eyes and handed it to her. She unlocked it and handed it back to him. He quickly downloaded the companion app from his laptop and opened it on Brin's phone.

A clicking noise came from the base of the exoskeleton as it established a connection with the phone app.

"This app talks to the exoskeleton, helping it maintain the right orientation and force vectors," James said as he handed the phone back to Brin. "It also gives it extra power. That's what that clicking noise was."

Brin nodded.

"This app should be open every time you wear your exoskeleton," James continued. "If you want to, you can just keep it open all the time. It won't drain your battery much at all." He gave her a hard look. "If your battery has any charge, that is."

"Right," Brin said, ignoring the barb. "Good to know."

"Okay," said James, standing up and stepping back. The giddy, hyperactive feeling came back to him, all sense of calm gone now.

He was just plain excited.

"Stand up," he said. "Give it a try."

Brin pushed her chair back and reached for her crutches.

"No, no." James waved her off. "Leave the crutches."

Brin furrowed her brow at him, but gave it a try anyway, pushing herself upright with one hand on the table and the other on the back of her chair. Once vertical, she found her balance and stood solid.

"How does that feel?" asked James. "Any pinching or discomfort?"

Brin shifted her weight a bit, back and forth.

"Nope," she said. "Feels good. Nice and tight, but not painful at all."

"Okay, great," James said.

He scurried behind her and pulled her chair away, then pushed the kitchen table toward the stove, giving Brin lots of room. She stood there in the center of the kitchen, wobbling slightly.

The exoskeleton looked like a giant ski boot with a cage on top of it. A bit too bulky, really. James would have to slim it down in the next design.

"Now, take it slow, at first," he said. "I want you to walk down the hallway. Toward the machine room."

"Okay," said Brin, drawing out the word. James could tell from her expression that she thought he was acting crazy.

But she still didn't know what the exoskeleton really did.

She shifted her weight to her good leg and swung forward the leg with the exoskeleton. She landed on the base of the boot and shifted her weight onto it.

James heard the servos spinning as she did so. The sensors were making ten thousand measurements per second, calculating the position of Brin's leg in space and sending adjustments to the servos to keep her body upright and her weight moving in the intended direction, always maintaining the stability of her injury.

But it did more than that.

As Brin rocked her weight from the heel of the exoskeleton to the toe and shifted back to her good leg, a dozen small plates on the foot of the exoskeleton pushed off in sequence with her, stablilizing her movement and adding force to it.

With this mechanism, Brin could step with her broken leg with ten times the strength and power of her good leg, but using a fraction of the energy.

It really was a bit like having a bionic leg.

"Holy fuck!" Brin said, as her bad leg shot forward with far more force than she would have been expecting. She took two stumbling steps down the hallway. The exoskeleton adjusted with her, preventing a fall and stabilizing her instantly with each step.

She stopped halfway down the hall, one hand against the wall, her chest heaving. She looked up at James.

James watched her carefully for some sign of what she was feeling. Was it too weird? Too uncomfortable for her? The power was truly an incredible extra-human enhancement. But some people weren't prepared for that and would reject it. Their minds would reject it as too artificial. Too inhuman.

Brin's eyes were wide with shock as she stared back at James.

Shit.

James gulped.

She hates it.

"Well?" he asked, preparing for the worst. "Is it okay?"

"Okay?" said Brin.

She grinned.

"It's fucking incredible."

27

BRIN SPENT the rest of the morning getting used to her exoskeleton. She learned how to balance while walking, turning, and standing from a sitting position. She learned how to walk up and down the stairs. With the exoskeleton, she could take the stairs even faster than she did with two fully healed legs.

Then she started to test the limits of the exoskeleton.

James assured her that the device was designed to maintain the safety and stability of her broken leg above all else. The base of the boot, he said, was designed with special sensors to anticipate upcoming shocks from footfalls and absorb the impact without transmitting the force into her bones.

As a result, when Brin walked, she felt like her leg was completely numb. No, numb wasn't the right word. She could feel the movement, but she didn't feel any impact. And yet her leg felt completely solid. It wasn't like when her leg fell asleep after keeping it in one position too long, where it felt numb and rubbery before the pins and needles set in. This felt strong and controlled, yet there was no sensation of the bones in her foot meeting the ground. It was an extremely odd feeling.

And once she got used to it, it was fantastic.

She started with the stairs, pushing off with the exoskeleton.

After a little practice, she could take the stairs two steps at a time, then three steps at a time. Then, she found that she could jump five steps with her bad leg, then two with her good leg, then five with her bad leg and she would be at the top of the stairs.

She felt like Superwoman, leaping a flight of stairs in a single bound.

Next, she tried running. First, she ran straight lines up and down the hallway. The hallway was maybe fifty feet from end to end. On her third try, she was covering the distance from a standstill in three strides.

These gadgets would definitely be banned from the Summer Olympics.

Her last test was for cornering. The hallway ran around the floor more or less in a rectangle, moving from the kitchen around two corners to the library, then around another corner to the office and machine room, then back around to the kitchen.

She banged into the walls a few times, sliding a bit on the slick tile floors. She gave herself a good stinger on her shoulder once or twice until James did something to the base of the boot to give her more traction. After that, she was flying around the loop, faster and faster. In only seven or eight strides she was motoring around the entire loop.

She felt invincible.

"This is incredible, James," she said breathlessly after completing one circuit. Then a mischievous thought entered her mind.

"Let's go outside," she said.

James laughed and led the way.

Brin found that the leg provided just as much stability on the soft forest floor as it had inside on the tile. When her foot sank into the soil, the exoskeleton would compensate to keep her upright. When her foot slid laterally on dead leaves or a patch of moss, the servos would adjust to help her maintain her balance.

It was a miraculous device.

She finally took a break for a sip of water from a bottle James brought out to her. Sweat was dripping off her nose and stinging her eyes. She was definitely going to need a shower. As Brin sipped, she started to think through the ramifications of James' incredible invention.

"James," she said, "you've got to sell these. This is a miracle device. People with broken bones, muscle injuries, maybe even people who've been paralyzed. They could all benefit from these. Not to mention the healthy people who will want them just for the added power. Construction workers will use them. Athletes. Elderly people. You'll make a fortune."

James smiled wanly and shook his head.

"That's not why I made it, Brin," he said. "I made it for you, to help you get out of here and back to civilization."

The tone of his voice and the look on his face were so sincere that Brin nearly teared up. This man, a man who Brin had only met a few days ago, had created one of the greatest medical devices of their time and didn't even think once about what it could do for him. He only thought about what it could do for Brin.

James was truly one of a kind. Brin had always thought he was weird. And he was. In the very best way.

Brin tipped her head back to drain her water bottle. As she swallowed, she looked up at the clouds breaking up before a blue sky, at the trees covered in moss, at the rock ledge above the house from which she'd fallen.

Another mischievous thought crossed her mind.

"What about jumping, James?"

"What about it?"

"Can I do it? Safely, I mean. Without screwing up my leg?"

James nodded.

"Sure," he said. "The sensors will detect your rate of descent and the proximity of the ground. The base of the boot will produce a force to counter the impact and deflect any additional force away from the leg."

Excited butterflies fluttered in Brin's chest. She tried to play it cool, nodding slowly, her face set in what she hoped was a thoughtful expression.

"And how high could I jump from?"

"I'd have to run some tests to be sure," said James. "I haven't really thought about that specific application before."

"Just ballpark, though," said Brin. "Five feet? Ten?" She eyed the ledge above the door. "Twenty?"

James scoffed.

"Oh, yeah. Please. That's nothing. This exoskeleton can generate at least five thousand pounds of force from the boot. For you, that's more like a forty foot jump, if I had to guess."

Brin couldn't contain the butterflies any longer. They came out as a huge grin on her face. She crunched the empty plastic water bottle in one hand, dropped it on the ground, and strode to stand on the flagstones in front of the door.

The same stones she'd faceplanted on three days earlier.

Brin squatted and swung her arms, then stood and did it again in a swinging, bouncing rhythm.

"What are you doing?" asked James.

Brin fixed her eyes on the ledge high above her.

"I'm gonna jump up on that ridge," she said.

"No, you're not," James said, a note of panic in his voice.

"Oh, yes, I am," Brin said.

"Brin, please don't, said James. "I don't want you to get hurt."

"You just said I could jump forty feet."

"Well," James spluttered, "that was just an estimate. I'd need to do some tests to be sure."

"Okay, great," said Brin, still swinging and bouncing, readying her muscles for the jump. "Here's the first test."

She looked over her shoulder at James. He had his hand in his long, lush hair again, one hand on his hip, turning in slow circles and stuttering, his worried thoughts tripping over themselves trying to leave his mouth.

"At least try on a smaller ridge," he finally managed.

Brin just smiled and refocused on the ridge above her.

Swing, bounce.

Swing, bounce.

Swing, and...

Brin pushed off with all the force she could muster, using the momentum of her swinging arms to add to it.

She flew into the air with such speed and force that she flailed her arms trying not to spin backwards. She shot past the ridge and into the air so high that she could see the peak of the mountain over the trees.

She must have jumped at least thirty feet straight up from a total standstill.

Fortunately, she had jumped forward just enough that her trajectory landed her at the top of the ridge instead of falling all the way back down onto hard stone.

James had been right. This wasn't the best place for her first ever bionic leap.

But she did it.

She let out a loud whoop and laughed at the sky. She walked to the edge of the ridge and looked down at James. His face had lost all color, but when Brin appeared at the top of the ridge, he seemed visibly relieved.

Brin held her arms out to her sides.

"Test successful, James," she said. She clapped her hands and whooped again.

Forget the broken leg. Brin hadn't felt this energized, this alive in years.

She stepped casually off the edge and dropped twenty feet. She barely felt the landing on her broken leg.

Incredible.

She pointed at James.

"James, you're a genius." She walked to him and kissed him full on the mouth.

His face had looked stunned before. It looked even more so now.

Brin swung her arm toward the front door to the house.

"Come on," she said. "Drinks are on me."

28

JAMES WAS WORRIED as he stood outside the house watching Brin walk inside with no crutches, her gait perfectly natural. He pushed his hand through his hair and sighed. Closing his eyes, he took a deep breath to calm himself. The rich smell of the forest and the crisp coolness of the air always soothed him. After a few more deep breaths, he was thinking more rationally.

Brin was pushing herself too hard. She had a broken leg, after all, and the exoskeleton was only designed to get her down the mountain, not make her into a superhero.

That said, James was also incredibly excited. The unit was performing far beyond even his wildest hopes. Part of it was due to Brin's strength, flexibility and natural athleticism. But there was no doubt that the exoskeleton was not only stabilizing and protecting her injured leg, but enhancing her physical abilities, as well.

She'd jumped thirty feet straight up in the air, for fuck's sake. James had envisioned any number of catastrophic outcomes before she left the ground, from her impaling herself on a tree branch or crushing her skull against the ridge on the way up to simply torquing mid-leap and landing on her skull on the flagstones again. She was lucky the first time. She wasn't likely to be so lucky again.

But, instead, she'd performed brilliantly.

And the exoskeleton had performed brilliantly.

The test was astounding to watch and more astounding to comprehend. For a fully healthy person, it would have been incredible. For someone with a broken leg, it was jaw-dropping.

And definitely worthy of a drink to celebrate.

And that kiss.

It was spontaneous, of course. Brin hadn't thought twice about it, James was sure.

But it had sent a jolt of energy through his entire body.

It made him want more than just a drink to celebrate.

When he walked into the kitchen, Brin was nowhere to be found. Then he heard noises coming from the wine room.

"I'm not much of a sommelier, James," Brin said when he came into the doorway of the pantry. She gestured to the rows of red wine bottles in curved wooden racks in front of her. "I really don't know what's good in here."

"Everything's good," said James, "but I don't really know much more than that." He walked through the pantry to stand at the door to the wine room, his arms folded, leaning against the doorjamb. "I hired someone to stock it for me. Told them Carrie's favorite wines and let them do the rest."

James looked around the small room. A wall of reds on the wall to his left. A large cooler of whites against the wall to his right. Some rosès and blends in between.

Most of the bottles were covered in a thin layer of dust. Before the other night, James hadn't even stepped foot in that room.

The other night.

James' heart froze as he looked down and saw the unopened bottle of port on the tasting table.

Unopened, and full of flunitrazepam.

He grabbed the bottle instinctively, his mind racing for a place to hide it before Brin turned her head.

She turned her head.

"Oh shit," she said, a smile lighting up her face, "is that the port we had the other night?"

She came and took the bottle from James.

"I thought you said we didn't have any more."

James shrugged and mumbled something unintelligible. His brain was freaking out. Just yesterday, he'd been willing to tell Brin everything, to come clean even though he knew she would hate him for it. Precisely because she would hate him for it, actually.

Now, after the excitement with the exoskeleton—and that spontaneous kiss—he would rather just forget he'd ever thought of that stupid plan to drug Brin. Just pretend it didn't happen.

"I don't know what you just said," said Brin, laughing, "but I do know that this stuff," she held up the bottle, "tastes damn good."

She moved past him in the doorway, brushing her body against James as she did so, holding his eyes with her own, gorgeous green pools that stopped James' heart every time. Her touch sent more jolts of energy through his body.

He quickly dampened that energy with self-hatred.

She's literally carrying a bottle of poison. If she drank too much of that, she would die.

Okay, she'd pass out from drunkenness long before she drank enough to die, but it was still theoretically possible.

And it was all because of James and his unbelieveable, thick-headed, anti-social selfishness.

Stupid. Stupid. Stupid.

She deserves better. Much, much better.

"Brin," James called as he came out of the pantry into the kitchen.

Brin was reaching up into the cabinets by the stove to grab

two port glasses. Her stretch lifted her shirt enough to reveal her bare waist. Memories shot into James' mind. Memories of Brin's body, her body against his, caressing each other.

He shook his head sharply to bring back his focus.

"You know," said Brin over her shoulder, "if you could get this exoskeleton thing to lift up like an elevator when I'm trying to reach high shelves, I think that'd be a great improvement."

"Brin, we can't drink that port."

She finally managed to finesse two glasses from the cabinet and set them on the counter beside the bottle of port. James could see that she'd already peeled off the wax that covered the stopper.

"Why not?" Brin said. "Come on. We're celebrating."

James wanted to tell her right then. He wanted to come clean with her, admit the whole devious plot. But he pictured her face when he told her. He pictured the revulsion, the incredulity, the lack of all respect she might have had for James.

Right now, she was giddy with happiness. She was wearing the exoskeleton that James had designed and fabricated and she was full of admiration and gratitude for him.

James wanted to tell her.

But, he couldn't bring himself to do it.

Not right then.

"Come on," said Brin, pulling the kitchen table back into the center of the room from where James had moved it to make room for Brin's exoskeleton track and field event.

She pulled one of the kitchen chairs over and patted it with her hand.

"Sit down," she said. "We're gonna celebrate this... this..." She seemed to struggle to find the right word as she pulled over the second kitchen chair. "...this victory. This breakthrough."

Her smile lit up her face. She was so excited, so positive. James could feel her energy, could feel it trying to lift him from his deep funk.

"That's what this is, James," she said. "It's a fucking medical breakthrough."

She was right. This was a breakthrough. And he had done it himself in this house in the middle of the woods. He'd made the designs, created the 3-D models, fabricated the parts, and assembled the exoskeleton. He'd written the software that controlled it. He'd worked out all of the math and all of the physics and he'd done it all by himself without a lab, without research assistants, without any help at all.

It was a breakthrough. It was cause for celebration.

But when Brin brought the port bottle from the counter and set it on the table with the two glasses, the thump of the bottle on the table was like the gavel of a judge, sentencing James to life in prison and an afterlife in hell for his selfishness.

There was no celebration in him.

Brin was still in danger.

Maybe not from her injuries, but from the killer who could be looking for her.

And from James.

"No, Brin," said James. He swept the port bottle off the table and dropped it in the garbage can.

"What the fuck, James," Brin said, shaking her head. "What is wrong with you?"

"The port is... bad," he stammered, hating himself for yet another lie. "It's no good. It's... expired."

A bad lie at that.

He was a coward. A liar and a coward.

"Expired?" said Brin. "We just drank some last night."

James shook his head.

"This is from... an older batch," he said.

He had to change the subject. With each successive lie, his shame grew deeper and deeper. He couldn't bear it any longer. He couldn't even look Brin in the eye. She just sat there, slumped in her chair, looking confused, all excitement gone in the face of James' negativity.

"Look," said James, "I'm sorry. I think I'm just really tired or something."

"Right," said Brin. "Right, of course. You haven't slept in, what, thirty hours?" She stood and put her hand on his shoulder.

It sent both a shiver of excitement and a wave of self-loathing coursing through him. The last thing Brin should be feeling is kind toward James.

If she only knew the truth.

He had to tell her.

But, even as he thought it, he knew he wouldn't. He was too cowardly.

"Come on, James," said Brin. "Let's get you in bed."

She slid her arm around his shoulder and pulled him in close to her. James felt her hair cool against his cheek, the sweet smell of her shampoo mingling with the scent of her sweat. Again, memories of the other night flooded James' mind.

He wanted so desperately to just let go, to let Brin bring him to bed and then convince her to stay there with him. To forget reality and just retreat to that bliss with Brin.

"No," said James, jerking himself out of his seductive thoughts.

He also jerked himself out of Brin's embrace.

She held her hands in front of her, palms out.

"Woah, easy, James."

James risked a look at Brin's eyes. The hurt and confusion he found there burned his soul. His lies were causing Brin pain.

He needed to get her to safety.

He needed to get her away from that killer.

He needed to get her away from him.

29

James was driving Brin fucking crazy. She'd never met a guy who was so goddamn hot and cold. One minute, she's kissing him, feeling him leaning into her. The next minute he won't even look her in the eye.

She even practically threw herself at him. First she tried to get him to drink the port like they had the other night. Then she put her arm around him and was literally taking him to the bedroom.

She knew he had feelings for her. She could feel it coming off of him in waves.

And try as she might to dismiss him, Brin had to admit that she had feelings for him, too.

She was trying to write him off, trying to forget about him.

But he was still totally fucking hot.

And scenes from the other night kept popping into her head.

And into her body.

And he was the only other person in the house. She was completely dependent on him for everything.

Until he'd given her the exoskeleton. That thing was a fucking miracle. Suddenly, Brin felt completely unhindered by her broken leg. She even caught herself forgetting her leg was broken at all.

After a few hours of wearing it, Brin barely even noticed the exoskeleton anymore. She'd adjusted her stride and her movements to accommodate the extra bulk. And though she knew the thing was heavy, since she'd seen James muscling it onto her leg—and her memory of those muscles brought her right back to the other night, dammit—she didn't feel the weight at all when she walked. The exoskeleton completely compensated for its own weight and then some.

It was truly an incredible invention, and she couldn't understand why James wasn't as overjoyed about it as she was.

Instead, he was acting like a moody bitch.

He'd thrown away a perfectly good bottle of port. When she tried to get him into the bedroom, he'd jumped out of her arms like she'd stuck him with a cattle prod.

And then, right after saying he was dead tired from being awake through the night, he insisted on going out and setting up all the extra surveillance cameras.

It was nice that he cared so much about Brin's safety. But Brin would still rather have spent a few hours rolling in the sheets and *then* go set up the camera.

And he'd insisted that he go out alone. He wanted Brin to stay home and confirm that the cameras were transmitting and the feeds were coming up on the new screens that James had installed around the house.

So here Brin was, a miracle device strapped to her leg that made her practically invincible, feeling healthy for the first time in days, horny as fuck, alone in a remote house in the woods with a super-hot guy who was amazing in bed... and she was alone, staring at a black TV screen, with earbuds in her ears, waiting for James to check in with the first camera.

Brin almost wished she could just lay back down in her

hospital bed, get that IV set back up, drip some painkillers in, and just sleep until the world made sense again.

"Brin, you copy?" said James over the earpods.

You copy?

What a fucking boy scount. Like a little kid with his walkie talkie.

Brin couldn't help but grin.

"Roger, that, Eagle One," Brin replied. "Red Phoenix copies, over and out."

James didn't reply for a moment.

"Very funny," he said.

Brin grinned again. Maybe this could be fun after all.

"First camera is mounted and secure," said James. "Powering up now."

"Roger that, Little Einstein," said Brin. "10-4, over."

"Great," said James, drily. "You should see a video feed come up in a few seconds."

"Standing by for visual, over."

The TV screen flickered once and an image came up on the screen. It was a view facing down from the crook of a tree. James appeared in a fisheye lens, his nose comically large, his eyes concentrated, his hands on either side of the screen, adjusting the camera.

"Eyes on, Port Killer," said Brin, "we are go for visuals, 10-4, over and out, roger."

In the video feed, Brin saw James' big-nosed face pull back, replaced center screen with his middle finger.

"Copy that, Salty Bear," she said, "Camera #1 is operational."

She watched James walk off screen.

Radio silence.

"Are you gonna do that the whole time?" he finally asked.

Brin managed to hit the mute button, then laughed so hard she may have peed in her pants. Just a little.

Still, James deserved it for being such a moody prick all morning.

"We'll see," she said into the microphone once she'd gathered herself again.

They continued in this fashion for hours. James would give Brin the heads up, she'd watch his face appear in a new video feed on the monitor, then he'd move on to the next location. With each feed, Brin could see the shadows growing longer and longer behind James.

"Just a couple more," said James. "Getting closer to the trailhead, so there might be some people."

He was right. When he brought up the next feed, Brin could see a blue jacket moving through the trees behind James. How wide was he making his surveillance loop? It almost looked like he was back up to the trail where Brin had seen the murder occur.

"Well, yeah," said James when Brin asked him about it. "I want to know if that guy comes back to the site looking for you."

It made sense. But why not just take Brin with him and leave the forest altogether. With the exoskeleton, the ridge above the house was no longer an obstacle. And even if it was, she could easily make the journey around it the long way, like James had done with the cameras.

It was starting to feel to Brin like James was acting irrationally. Like there were obvious solutions that they weren't following for some reason.

Like right now. Why put up all the cameras? Brin was mobile again. Why not just hike out of the woods to safety? Odds are that the killer didn't even see Brin and wasn't looking for her at all.

Brin shivered when she pictured again that moment in the woods. The shaved head. The stubbled beard. The tattoo on his neck. His face so emotionless when he pulled that trigger.

Like he'd done it a hundred times before.

Brin heard the gunshot again in her mind. It still stopped her heart.

"Brin? You still there?"

Brin shook herself back to reality.

"Uh, yeah," she said. "Sorry. I'm here."

"We good?" said James.

"What? Of course we're good," Brin said. "Why wouldn't we be good?"

Why was he asking that?

"I mean the video feed," James said. "Is the video feed transmitting?"

"Oh," said Brin, feeling foolish for having spaced out.

She checked the monitor and saw James' boots in the bottom of a new video feed that had appeared on the screen, dead leaves and green moss all around them.

"Looks good," Brin said.

"Okay," said James. "Last one, then."

Suddenly, Brin was glad that James was putting up the cameras and grateful to him for his caution and his compassion. He could just take her out of the forest. He could just send her on her way, leave her to fend for herself.

Hell, he could have just left her unconscious on his doorstep.

But, here he was, still helping her. He'd built her this incredible device and he'd spent hours in the woods mounting cameras to keep her safe, all on the basis of a memory, a story she'd told him. He didn't know if it was true. He was just trusting her.

Trusting her and going to extraordinary lengths based on that trust.

"Okay, almost set with the last camera," James said. "You ready?"

Brin reset her focus. She was sticking with James all the way to the end. He trusted her. She was going to trust him, too.

"Ready when you are," she said.

The last camera feed flickered to life in the lower corner of the monitor, one of nearly thirty small boxes filling the screen, each showing a different part of the forest.

Again, she saw James' fisheyed nose in the picture, his arms up to the sides, adjusting the camera.

Then she saw two feet come into the background, underneath James' armpit in the frame.

Boots. Men's boots.

Not hiking boots, though. Black leather, like work boots, but nicer.

"James, I think someone is behind you," said Brin softly into the microphone.

She saw James turn his head to look over his shoulder.

"Oh, hello," he said to the person.

Brin heard the man's voice, low-pitched, but muffled. She couldn't make out what he was saying.

"Bird watching, actually," she heard James say.

He finished adjusting the camera, looked square into it.

Looked straight at Brin.

He squeezed his lips into a thin line and nodded once. He touched the earpod in his ear and the audio went dead.

Brin was thrown by the sudden silence. Why would James disconnect the audio?

Though she could no longer hear anything, Brin could still see through the video feed.

When James put down his arms and moved away from the camera, the man behind him came into view.

Brin's heart stopped again.

Icy fingers of fear ran up her throat.

It was the killer.

The man with the shaved head and the neck tattoo.

Chatting with James on the video feed right in front of her.

Brin screamed.

30

James recognized the man from Brin's description as soon as he looked over his shoulder at him.

He'd been wondering when some curious hiker would interrupt him and ask what he was doing. He'd even anticipated a conscientious Oregonian challenging his right to put up cameras in the forest.

He had permits for all of the surveillance he'd set up around his house, of course, but these new cameras were technically illegal.

But, James had his cover story all ready, so he wasn't too worried when Brin had warned him about his visitor.

Until he had looked over his shoulder.

There in the dead leaves, wearing a zipped-up black leather jacket, black jeans, and black boots, looking like he had just stepped out of a New York deli and into the forests of Oregon, was the man Brin had described.

The killer.

"That some kind of camera?" said the man in response to James' greeting.

The man's voice was gravelly and he had an accent that actually sounded like it could have been from New York. He had his hands stuffed into the pockets of his jacket, making two little bulges in front of his belly.

Bulges that could have concealed a gun.

"What you setting up cameras out here in the woods for, huh?" asked the man.

"Bird watching, actually," replied James, trying to keep his voice light.

He turned back to the camera to give Brin some kind of silent signal, something to at least prepare her for what she would inevitably see as soon as James stepped away. A grim smile and a slight nod was all he could come up with.

Then he shut down the audio feed. The last thing he wanted was for the man to somehow hear Brin's voice echoing from James' earpods while James was working through his cover story.

"Birds, huh?" said the man. "Shouldn't the camera be pointed up, then?"

The man grinned. If he was trying to seem amiable or set James at ease, he was definitely not succeeding. The man was a predator. Every instinct in James' body was warning him to run. When the man grinned, all James could picture was him feeding off of James' dead flesh.

"Not many birds flying down here on the ground," said the man.

"That's true," James smiled back at the man, trying to hide his abject terror.

The man was as Brin had described: shaved head, dark stubble, tattoo on his neck. Only the tattoo wasn't a dragon. It looked more like some kind of angel, with its wings curling up around the man's neck.

"But," James continued with his cover story, "we're actually hoping to record the feeding behavior of *Pipilo maculatus*, more commonly known as the Spotted Towhee." James did his best to sound like an overexcited bird nerd. "It tends to feed on the ground, looking for seeds or other food items that have fallen amongst the underbrush."

He had researched the bird last night during a break while building Brin's exoskeleton. He'd switched the wi-fi back on so he could search the web for local ground feeders.

The man nodded slowly.

"You, uh, some kind of scientist or something?" he said.

"Ph.D. candidate, actually," said James.

He was riffing now, but felt on fairly solid ground. He had gotten his own Ph.D. when he was twenty-one years old.

"I'm writing my thesis on the ecology and ecosystem of ground feeding fauna in the Pacific Northwest," he continued, "with a special focus on ground-feeding avian species."

He was hoping to either scare the guy off with big, scientific words or simply bore him enough for him to walk away.

It seemed like the boredom route might have been working.

"Right, right," said the man, looking around the forest, seeming to lose interest in James. "Well, good luck with that then, professor."

"Thanks," replied James as the man walked away.

James tried to hide his relief, but his heart was pounding so hard he was sure the veins in his neck were pulsing visibly. He could feel his pulse in his temples like someone was squeezing his head with giant calipers over and over.

He quickly made sure he had all of his tools and equipment in his sling bag and walked away, trying his best to maintain a casual, normal walking speed.

All he really wanted to do was sprint away. Icy fear clawed up his throat and tingled his spine. It took all of James' willpower to slow his stride and maintain his composure.

He went in the opposite direction of the man, but was sure to move in a direction that led away from his house, from Brin, just in case the man thought to follow.

Once he felt like he'd gone far enough to throw the man off,

he looked carefully around the woods. Shadows were length-
ening and the air was starting to take on the chill of evening.
The orange glow of the lowering sun suffused the greens and
browns of the trees, leaves, and moss, lending an otherworldly
glow to the scene.

But James saw no sign of the killer. Or of anyone else, for
that matter.

James was alone.

He changed course and headed straight for home.

Straight for Brin.

31

BRIN'S MIND was freaking out as she watched the small box on the screen, watched James in the video feed talking to the man she'd seen murder someone in the forest a few days ago.

Both James and the killer were standing in profile, their mouths moving silently. The killer had his hands stuffed into his pockets like a thug on a bad cop show.

In the afternoon sunlight, dappling the forest tableau around them—trees and moss and fallen leaves and dark soil—they looked like two dads chatting after their kids' soccer game.

If one of the dads was a murderer.

Brin watched the man eye James. He seemed to be evaluating him, deciding whether or not James was of any interest.

James, for his part, seemed to be his usual nerdy self. Brin didn't know what he was saying, something about bird watching, she supposed, since that was the last thing she'd heard. But he looked just like he looked whenever he talked about his building machines or about Brin's medical status.

Nerdy and intense.

Pretty soon, the killer had the same look on his face that Brin probably had on hers during those conversations. The look of someone who wishes they hadn't asked whatever question had set James off. The look of someone desperately seeking a way out of the conversation.

Perfect.

Brin didn't know if James had anticipated this situation. Seemed unlikely, but she was far beyond selling James short for anything anymore. But, either way, he was playing it perfectly.

The killer's eyes, curious and suspicious at first, now were bored and darting, seeking escape. He said something dismissive, it seemed, and walked away.

James kept his cool. Brin had to admire him for that. She was absolutely freaking out, and she was far away from the killer. James, standing right in front of him, was calmly packing his bag before he strolled away in the opposite direction from the killer.

Even though James had left the frame, Brin stared at the video feed for a long time after that. She was looking for signs of James or the killer, but all she was seeing was her memory.

The clearing.

The killer.

The gun.

And all she could hear in her mind, over and over again, was that single piercing gunshot, like the crack of splitting wood or a sudden thunderclap.

She hadn't seen the shot. She was running away by the time the man pulled the trigger.

But she could hear it, and in her mind now the bullet was chasing her, following her flight through the woods.

Seeking her out.

She stared at the video feed, now showing only leaves and soil and moss and fallen branches.

But she saw herself.

In jeopardy.

"No!" shouted Brin, standing up so fast that her chair flew backwards against the wall.

She felt the power of the exoskeleton as she stood. The

power and the stability. She felt strong where a moment before she'd felt so weak, so helpless.

Another gift from James.

She wanted to go outside to wait for James to return, but she knew that was foolish and risky. If the killer was out there, there could be others. Members of his crew, if he had one.

But she couldn't just sit there and wait, either. She needed to do something. Something to keep her mind occupied.

Maybe she could do more laps with the exoskeleton.

Brin pulled out her phone to make sure it still had a charge. James had said his exoskeleton app used very little battery, but she wanted to be sure. The last thing she wanted was for the exoskeleton to stop working because her phone battery went dead. Then she'd just have a heavy weight on her broken leg.

She wasn't sure if that's how it worked, but she didn't want to find out.

She glanced in the upper corner of her screen and saw that the battery indicator had gone down from five percent to three percent.

Uses no power my ass.

Brin looked around the office and spotted a charging cable on James' desk. As she plugged her phone in and the screen lit up to indicate charging, something on the display caught her eye.

The wi-fi signal.

It had full bars.

She had a wi-fi signal here in the house.

But how was that possible? James had said there was no wi-fi. Was this something to do with the cameras? Was the phone somehow connecting to the cameras and thinking it was connected to the internet?

Her hands shaking, Brin swiped on her phone and tapped on her web browser. If she could get a web page to load, she was online again.

Something flashed on the monitors.

Brin looked up.

It was James.

She saw him on one of the video feeds. He moved in from the left side of the frame and moved out the right side.

Then he appeared on one of the other feeds.

He was coming home.

Relief flooded through Brin. She nearly fell to the floor as her muscles, which she hadn't even realized were clenched, suddenly relaxed.

She put her phone in her pocket and watched James move from feed to feed until he appeared right at the front door.

When he opened it, Brin was there to greet him.

32

JAMES WAS tired when he got home. He was feeling the long trek he'd taken to mount the new cameras. Plus he hadn't slept in nearly two days.

And he'd confronted a killer in the woods.

All in all, it had been an eventful afternoon.

But when he opened the front door and Brin threw her arms around him, there in the doorway, his fatigue instantly fell away. He felt Brin's body against his, every nerve tingling with her warmth and the press of her against him. He buried his face in her soft hair, breathing deep its sweet scent.

They held each other close, tight, for a long time. With his embrace, James willed Brin's body into his, like he could blend her cells with his, dissolve her into him and form one being if only he could hold her tight enough.

And she held him back just as hard.

He felt her biceps straining against his side, her hands spread wide across his back, gripping hard and pulling him close. His body responded to the grind of her hips against his.

Slowly, slowly, their heads turned. James looked into Brin's eyes, those endless green eyes. They were soft and shining with passion. James' fatigue was quickly replaced by a hunger that consumed him.

James' body was already responding. Now his mind did too, letting go of all of the guilt and self-hate, giving in to the passion and love he felt for this incredible woman who had fallen into his life.

Their lips met and James' world melted away. Nothing mattered, nothing existed except his body and Brin's. Every touch, every movement, every sigh or moan was electric to James.

Through the foyer, down the hallway, into the bedroom, shedding clothes as they went.

Then toppling onto the bed, toppling into bliss, into help-lessness.

Toppling into heaven.

33

BRIN LAY IN BED, staring up at the ceiling, lit softly by a single bedside lamp. James lay beside her, still breathing hard. Their naked bodies were slick with sweat.

Brin hadn't been thinking about sex when she threw her arms around James after he got home.

Not consciously, at least.

But, the raw emotion of the day had flooded out of her in that moment when she held him. She'd held him so tight and so close, wishing with all her heart that she would never have to let him go.

And he held her back just as hard.

When she felt his body responding to their embrace, her own thoughts moved beyond companionship and on to something more... intimate.

For an hour or so, all of her fears and worries had faded away. She'd lost all sense of time and space. There was only James. Nothing else in the world.

James and the mindblowing ecstasy of being with him.

Mind blown and body spent, she lay staring up at the ceiling.

"Welcome back," she said.

James chuckled softly.

"If that's how you greet me," he said, "I'll leave more often."

Brin rolled over and kissed James' chest.

"How about we skip the leaving and just cut right to the welcome?"

As she did so, James' stomach growled. Loud.

James put his hand on his belly.

"Sorry," he said, embarrassed. "Guess I'm hungry."

At mention of the word, Brin realized how long it had been since she'd eaten.

"Me, too," she said. "I'm starving."

She scooted to the edge of the bed, looking on the floor for her clothes. She settled for James' undershirt. When she stood and pulled it on, it covered her naked bum, but only barely.

"I could watch you wear that outfit all day," James said.

Brin posed seductively for him and laughed when she saw his penis grow hard.

"Hang on there, tiger," she said. "I love your enthusiasm, but what say we eat something before Round Two?"

She looked down at the exoskeleton on her leg.

"My phone's in the office charging," she said. "Is this thing gonna work?"

James rolled over on his side and stretched long on the bed. In the dim golden lamp light, his long hair draped seductively over one eye, the shadows fell over his biceps, his stomach muscles, his butt and legs in a way that almost made Brin forget all about food and get Round Two started right away.

He closed his eyes like he might fall asleep right there. Brin kept forgetting how long James had been awake. He needed to eat and go to sleep.

After Round Two, of course.

"It'll still work," he mumbled. "Won't be as stable without the signal from the phone."

He propped himself up on one elbow, looking so gorgeous in the light that Brin's heart skipped a beat.

"And you can't jump over the house without the phone, either," James continued. "Without the added information from the phone, it's too dangerous to use full power, so it dials itself back to human levels. Until you're charged and back in bluetooth range," he grinned, "no more Super Brin."

"Super Brin," Brin smiled. "I like the sound of that."

She did, too. The feeling she had this morning was unlike anything she'd ever felt. When she ran around the house, ran outside, and especially when she jumped, she'd felt invincible.

"I'll pull some food together," she said, turning toward the hallway.

She was thinking about invincibility, about food, about the kitchen where she and James had kissed for the first time. She thought about her phone and the added power it would give when it finished charging.

"Oh," she said, remembering, "I noticed something weird when I plugged in the phone earlier."

She stopped and turned back to face James.

"There was a wi-fi signal on my phone."

James had been smiling, but his face fell when she said that, his brow furrowed.

A chill suddenly went through Brin.

She was overreacting, though. There had to be a perfectly reasonable explanation.

But after years of bad boyfriends, Brin had learned to trust her gut. And right now, her gut felt rotten.

"James," Brin said, trying her best to keep her voice from sounding accusatory or agitated, "why would there be a wi-fi signal on my phone?"

James sat up and slid to sit on the edge of the bed, his back to Brin. He pulled his pants on and stood, barefoot and shirtless, in only his jeans.

Despite the chill that Brin still felt, despite the rotten feeling in her gut, she couldn't help thinking it.

James was a damn fine-looking man.

"Brin," James said, "there's something I've been meaning to tell you."

In Brin's experience, those words never led to a pleasant conversation.

In her experience, those words almost always led to a knock-down, drag-out, blood-on-the-floor fight.

She steeled herself for the hammer blow.

34

James was kicking himself.

After researching local ground feeding birds for his cover story while hanging cameras, he'd forgotten to turn the wi-fi off again. He'd been so tired from staying up all night and the adrenaline from building the exoskeleton that he'd just forgotten to turn it off.

Or maybe it was his subconscious purposely trying to get him to own up to his own bullshit. Maybe he had sabotaged himself so he would be forced to come clean with Brin.

He stood there in the bedroom, wearing only a pair of jeans. Brin was dressed only in James' undershirt, an old light grey college t-shirt, worn very thin from years of use.

Thin enough to be almost see-through.

Brin's long red hair curled over her breasts. Her long legs were bare well up her thighs, covered only by the cast and the exoskeleton on one leg.

James wanted nothing more than to have a quick bite to eat and to fall back into bed with Brin. It made no sense to him, how quickly he'd fallen for this woman. In only a matter of days, he suddenly couldn't imagine life in this house without her. Without clomping around downstairs or making coffee or laying on the couch in the library sketching the room. He couldn't imagine her not sleeping in the bed beside him. He couldn't imagine not seeing her green eyes and shining smile every day.

Couldn't, or just didn't want to.

Because he knew he wouldn't have it. He knew he wasn't even close to good enough for Brin.

And now she would know it, too.

"I just want to say from the start," James began, "that your safety, your health, was always the most important consideration for me."

He couldn't keep eye contact with her. He felt too guilty. But he risked a glance to see her reaction.

She was just waiting, revealing nothing in her expression.

"I would never do anything to harm you," James said. "I hope you know that."

"James," said Brin, "what are you talking about? You've done nothing but amazing things for me from the moment I fell on your doorstep."

James winced. Brin's words were like a needle prick to his heart. It would be better for him if she already thought he was an asshole. Then he wouldn't be letting her down.

Then he wouldn't be losing so much.

Still, he couldn't wait any longer. Couldn't lie again. Now was the time for James to come clean.

"The reason your phone had a wi-fi signal," James began, "is because... I do have wi-fi in this house. I've had it all along."

Brin's brow furrowed and she closed her eyes, seeming to process what James had just said. She shook her head.

"Wait," she said, "what about the other day, when you said you didn't have signal or wi-fi."

James nodded.

"I did say that," he admitted. "I lied. I'm... so sorry."

"But my phone really didn't have a signal," Brin said. "When

I looked at it then, there was nothing. No bars for cellular. Nothing for wi-fi."

"Well, there really is no cellular signal here," James explained. "We're in the middle of the woods."

"Okay," said Brin. "But the wi-fi bit was a lie?"

James took a deep breath and pulled his hand through his hair.

"I turned it off when you woke up that first day," he said. "I knew your phone would be the first thing you asked for when you were feeling better again."

"So you turned off the wi-fi," Brin said.

"Right."

"And lied to me about it."

"I'm so sorry, Brin."

She shook her head, looking confused.

"Okay," she said, drawing out the word. "And then you turned it back on again?"

James was tempted to lie again, to say he'd had a change of heart or his conscience had gotten the better of him. But, no. He was coming clean with Brin and he was gonna come all the way clean, whatever the consequences.

"I didn't mean to," he said. "I was looking up something online last night and forgot to turn it back off."

Brin laughed at that, still shaking her head. She wandered in a small circle, shaking her head, gesturing with her hands, like she was having a conversation in her head.

"Okay," she said, looking at James.

James' heart stopped for a moment.

"Okay?" he said.

"Yeah, okay," Brin replied. "Whatever. I mean, it wasn't a cool thing to do. My friends are probably freaking out wondering what happened to me. But," Brin gestured to her leg, "it's a small thing compared to everything you've done for me, James."

James' heart started again, now skipping a beat.

She'd forgiven him.

He'd come clean and she'd forgiven him.

He could stop now and still have a wonderful night. A quick snack then back into bed with Brin.

But he hadn't come clean. Not all the way.

"Come on, James," said Brin, turning toward the hallway, "I'm starved. Let's get something to eat."

This was James' last chance to just sweep everything under the rug and pretend it never happened.

But if he did that and everything worked out perfectly with Brin, if they started a long relationship together, it would be based on a lie. A lie of omission.

He didn't want to do it like that. Brin deserved better. She deserved to make her own choices.

She deserved to know the truth.

"Brin, wait," he said.

Brin stopped in the hallway and turned back to him.

"There's one other thing I haven't told you yet," James said.

35

THIS NIGHT WAS NOT GOING the way Brin had been hoping.

Brin didn't like lies. At all. She'd had too many bad boyfriends—including Evan, the most recent—lie to her face.

She was sick of it.

She wasn't going to put up with it anymore.

But, for some reason, she was willing to let the issue with the wi-fi go.

She surprised herself when she realized she didn't really care. When James had confessed to the lie, Brin knew she should be pissed off. She knew she should chew James out.

But she was pacing in circles in the bedroom.

On a broken leg.

After a very bad fall.

Wearing some kind of miracle prosthetic, the exoskeleton.

She didn't know why James had chosen to lie about the wi-fi, but he'd done so much good for her in the last few days that she was willing to forgive and forget on this one.

And there was something between them. Some kind of connection that Brin hadn't felt before. The sex was unbelievable, sure. But there was something more. Something deeper.

For the sake of that deeper connection, Brin was willing to overlook the wi-fi issue.

But now James said he had more to tell her.

In Brin's experience, the words *I have something I haven't told you yet* never ended with both people having a quick snack and tumbling back into bed together again.

She sighed, seeing her night slipping away.

"Okay, James," Brin said. "What is it? Did you upgrade my operating system without telling me?"

Brin was trivializing the wi-fi thing, which irked her even as she did it. She didn't want James to think it was okay to lie to her. But she would rather do all of this shit tomorrow.

There was always time for an argument.

"No," said James quietly.

Something about his tone pulled Brin out of her mini mental tantrum.

Whatever it was, this thing was really bothering James.

What the fuck did he do?

Brin had only been there for a couple of days. What could he possibly have done? The worst she could imagine was rape on the bed while she was unconscious after her fall. But she would have known if he did that.

Brin took a step toward James. He stepped backward in response, keeping distance between them.

His face was twisted in pain, like he was punishing himself by staying away from Brin.

Is this why he'd been so standoffish the other morning?

"What is it, James?" Brin said softly. "What's wrong?"

"It's the port," said James.

Brin hadn't been expecting that response.

But she remembered how weird James had acted about the port just that morning.

"What about it?" she said.

"You see," said James, "I built this place to be away from people. Isolated."

"Right," said Brin. "For Carrie to have some peace and quiet."

"Yes, at first," said James. "But when she died, I moved in so I could have that peace and quiet for myself."

He turned around, facing the wall and shaking his head.

"No, no," he muttered. "That's not the truth. Not the real truth."

He was acting like a mental patient, or like those tweaked out people on the street downtown who carry on full, animated conversations with themselves.

James spun suddenly and faced Brin again. His brown eyes were so intense, so earnest that Brin wanted to pull him into her arms and tell him everything would be okay.

"Not peace and quiet," he said. "That's not why I moved in here."

He paced back and forth in front of Brin.

"I came here," he continued, "to isolate myself. I wanted never to see another person again."

"You were grieving," said Brin. "You can't blame yourself for wanting some space to heal."

"No, no, that's not the point," James said, shaking his head. "For three years, I didn't see anyone. I didn't talk to anyone. By design, you see?"

He looked at her, his expression pleading.

She didn't quite understand why this was so important, but she nodded, trying to help James.

He saw right through her. His frustration showed on his face.

"I didn't want to be found," he said. "By anyone. Ever again."

He was trying so hard to communicate something that Brin felt obligated to try harder to understand it.

"You wanted to be alone," Brin said.

James nodded.

"You wanted to be out here all alone. To grieve. To heal."

"Yes, yes, but more than that," James said. "I wanted to hide, Brin. I wanted to hide and never be found."

Was this what he was so upset with himself about?

"There's nothing wrong with that, James," she said. "You don't need to feel bad. Everyone wants to hide once in a while."

"Three years I've been here." James was nearly shouting. "Three years hidden. And I intended to stay hidden forever."

That sounded kind of extreme to Brin, but would James really have stuck with it? He probably would have come back to reality, eventually.

"And then you came in," said James.

"Fell in, you mean," Brin said, trying to lighten the mood. James had gone to a very dark place all of a sudden.

"And I couldn't just leave you there," James said. He was staring into space now, as if he had forgotten Brin was there.

As if he were talking to himself.

"I knew I could help you," he said. "I couldn't leave you there and I couldn't just dump you somewhere for 9-1-1 to pick up."

What the fuck? Had he really considered that?

"So I brought you inside. I took the films. I ran the tests. I patched you up."

Brin kept her mouth shut. A voice in the back of her mind was telling her something was very wrong, but she ignored it. She wanted to see where this was headed.

"But, I couldn't let you know where we were," James continued. "I couldn't let you tell anyone else where to find me, or let you lead them to me."

This was some paranoid shit. Why would Brin try to lead anyone back here?

"Those vultures out there. I couldn't let them find me again."

"What vultures, James?"

"The press," he said, eyes wide. "The money grubbers. They all just suck you dry, like vampires. Don't care about you at all."

He shook his head, staring into space again.

"I couldn't let them find me again," he continued. "So I had to get you out. Patch you up and get you out."

"Okay, James," Brin said, trying to soothe him. "You did that. You patched me up. And now, I can go."

Brin swallowed hard.

"If that's what you want," she said.

"But you woke up too soon," James continued, as if he hadn't heard Brin speak at all. "You were supposed to stay unconscious for another day or two."

The conversation was starting to take a sinister turn.

"James, maybe we can talk more tomorrow."

"But you woke up," he continued, "so I needed a way to get you out without you being aware of your surroundings."

Brin had been curious earlier about where this was all headed. But now she didn't want to know. A sick feeling was growing in the pit of her stomach.

"Okay, James," Brin said. "I'm going to go to bed, I think."

"The port, Brin," James said. "Don't you see? If you drank the port, you'd be unconscious and I could move you safely."

He looked in her eyes, touched her arm. Brin could feel his pain, could feel his desire, his need for her to understand. She could see it in the depths of his eyes.

"You were going to get me drunk?" she asked.

He took her other arm, held both in his hands. His grip wasn't tight, but it was firm. He squared her shoulders to his, looked deep into her eyes.

"Do you understand why I did it, Brin? Why I was going to do it?"

Brin's head was starting to hurt. The voice in the back of her mind grew louder. The skin on her neck tingled and itched. She wanted to be in a dark, quiet room for a while to process her thoughts and feelings.

"Because you wanted to be alone?" she guessed.

To be honest, she was having trouble following James' ramblings. First it was the wi-fi. Now this impassioned plea for her understanding, all because he wanted to be alone in the woods to grieve.

"Not alone," said James. "Hidden. I needed to stay hidden."

"Right," Brin remembered. "From the vultures."

James nodded slowly. His shoulders had been bunched around his ears, but now started to loosen, to lower.

"Yes," he said, sounding relieved. "That's why I did it."

"Did what, James?"

Brin couldn't keep the exasperation from her voice. Her headache was worsening by the second. Her nausea was growing. And the voice in her mind was rattling her skull with warning.

"What did you do?" she asked again.

"Flunitrazepam," he whispered. "In the port."

"Fluni... what is that? Some kind of drug?"

James swallowed hard and nodded.

"Rohypnol," he said.

Brin was stunned.

"The... date rape drug?" she said.

James looked away, avoiding her eyes again. He nodded.

Brin had heard stories of frat boys spiking drinks with Rohypnol and doing terrible things to women while they were unconscious. Mocking them. Degrading them. Hurting them. Defiling them.

Then posting it all on social media.

And still getting away with it.

Brin's headache spiked, but she focused the pain. Her fists coiled tightly. A dagger of ice formed in her chest.

"Were you planning to rape me, James?" Brin said, her voice low, barely controlled.

"No!" His eyes shot wide and he held his hands up before him. "No, no." He shook his head. "Absolutely not. Never."

"Then why, James? Why would you do that to me?"

"Just so I could move you," he said, "take you through the forest to the road. Call for help to pick you up."

"Why? Just so I wouldn't see your hiding place?"

Brin's anger mounted.

"You were going to drug me," she said, rage boiling in her voice, "and drag me unconscious through the woods at night."

She moved slowly toward James.

"With a broken leg."

James backed away, fear growing in his eyes.

"All so you could stay hidden here in the woods?"

Brin clenched her fists so tightly she heard her knuckles crack.

"You would knock me unconscious just so you wouldn't have to talk to reporters?"

She advanced on James like a lion stalking its prey.

"Is that what you're telling me?"

The fear in James' eyes suddenly turned to resignation.

To defeat.

"Yes," he choked. "Yes, that's right."

He sighed and lowered his head.

"I'm so sorry, Brin," he said. "I don't deserve you."

Brin had been ready to fight James. Ready to clock him. To knock him unconscious so he would know what it felt like to be helpless. To be at someone else's mercy.

Seeing him like that, though, with so much self-hate in his eyes, Brin's anger cooled. James was clearly in pain. Brin couldn't possibly beat him up any worse than he was already beating up himself.

And she no longer wanted to.

But she couldn't stand to look at him right then, either.

She turned and stalked out of the bedroom.

Her head was still spinning with what she'd heard.

What the fuck kind of person would drug someone unconscious so they could call 9-1-1? Who would be so messed up to do that just to hide their address?

Brin's mind was swimming with these thoughts. Her headache was pounding.

And the voice in the back of her mind was screaming.

As she stalked into the kitchen, the soft glow of the light above the stove was the only thing visible now that night had fallen. It seemed so dark and lonely and peaceful and quiet in there.

Then something pinched the sides of her neck.

Hard.

It pinched and squeezed.

It pulled her up short. Nearly pulled her off her feet.

"Hello, Red," said a gravelly voice quietly, hot breath in her ear.

Brin knew that voice.

It had been haunting her dreams for days.

Her anger disappeared.

Sheer panic took its place.

36

THE DEVASTATION JAMES felt was bottomless.

Like a deep, dank, dark well.

He felt himself slip into it, falling, drowning.

He deserved the despair. He deserved the pain.

He deserved every ounce of unhappiness that came his way.

He was a horrible person. A horrible, selfish person.

And now Brin knew it, too.

She knew what he had done and she agreed that it—that he—was horrible.

James just stood there in the bedroom, the clothes he and Brin had stripped off in the heat of passion strewn about the tile floor around his bare feet.

That passion felt years away.

That passion he didn't deserve.

And would never feel again.

The colors of the room faded to grey. The golden glow of the lights. The colors of the clothes. All faded to grey dullness.

And James was fading with it.

Falling into that well.

Falling into that bottomless devastation.

He heard a loud crash and a grunt.

It sounded like it had come from the kitchen.

Had Brin hurt herself? Had she tried to get something from the top shelf and slipped? Or pulled whatever she was reaching for down on top of herself?

She'd asked James to modify the exoskeleton to lift her when she reached for upper shelves. He hadn't had a chance to work on it yet.

And now she could be hurt.

There was always room for more reasons to hate himself, but self-flagellation could come later.

Right now, James had to make sure Brin was all right.

He jogged out of the bedroom and down the hallway to the kitchen, padding along softly and swiftly on his bare feet. There was a soft glow at the end of the corridor, coming from the kitchen.

Then that glow was darkened by a figure.

Not Brin's figure.

This figure was much larger. A man's figure.

By the time this fact registered in James' brain, he'd already come out of the corridor toward the kitchen. He saw more clearly now a man's back, broad under a black leather jacket.

In the glow from the kitchen light, he could see a tattoo on the man's neck.

He was hunching over something on the floor.

Garbage was strewn everywhere. Bits of breakfast, coffee grounds. The port bottle. The garbage can was on its side, the lid still rolling crazily toward the wall.

And Brin.

Brin was on the floor.

The man stopped moving toward her. He started to look behind him.

Toward James.

James darted to his right, down the side corridor toward the library.

He didn't think the man had seen him, but he had to assume he knew James was there. In the house somewhere.

How long had the man been there?

How had he gained entry to the house?

How had he even found the house?

These questions flew through James' mind as he darted down the hallway, then through the library and around into his office.

But he didn't have time to worry about them now.

All that mattered was the here and now.

The facts of the present moment.

The killer had found them.

And Brin was in trouble.

37

"HELLO, RED."

Brin's subconscious recognized the voice before her conscious mind could catch up. A chill ran up her spine and a cold clammy sweat broke out over her whole body.

The killer.

He had her by the neck, squeezing harder and harder.

The chill in her spine turned to pain as the man closed his gloved hands around her neck from behind.

"Not gonna get away this time," the man said into Brin's ear. His voice was low, his breath close and hot on her ear.

It brought the chill shivering over her body again.

He tightened his grip on Brin's neck even more. Pain speared Brin's neck, up into her head. Her headache bloomed like a mushroom cloud within her skull.

The killer lifted Brin, stretching her neck until only the tips of her toes brushed the kitchen floor. Brin couldn't move. She felt helpless.

And terrified.

The killer threw her.

Shoved her with force forward, down the hallway at an angle.

Brin flew into the wall, her shoulder taking the brunt of the impact.

Pain stabbed through her shoulder and her arm went numb for a moment.

She ricocheted off the wall, fell into the trash can. It tipped and she fell on top of it on the floor, knocking the wind out of her before she bounced off of it onto the floor.

Brin gasped and coughed, struggling to catch her breath.

She took a quick inventory of her body. Aside from flaring pain in her shoulder and a fiery ring of pain around her neck, she was okay. It didn't feel like any bones had broken.

She was on her stomach, surrounded by the contents of the trash can: dirty paper towels, coffee grounds, the port bottle, and scraps from breakfast.

She crawled forward, pulling herself through the trash with her elbows, like a soldier under fire.

"Mmmm," said the killer behind her. "I do like that. Might have to kill you a little later than scheduled."

Brin realized then that she was wearing only a t-shirt.

Crawling on the floor on her stomach, she was completely exposed to the killer.

Tears flooded Brin's eyes, unbidden.

Pull yourself together, Brin. Don't fall apart now.

She'd dealt with disgusting slimeballs before. She could do it again.

She kept crawling, focusing on catching her breath and moving forward, away from the killer.

Brin heard a metallic scrape and click behind her.

Like the cocking of a gun.

"Need to slow you down a bit first," said the killer.

Brin pushed the panic away.

She set her jaw, steeled herself, and rolled over to face the killer.

He leered at her, his eyes scanning up her body as it lay on the floor. A chilling grin spread across his face as he leveled his gun toward her.

Behind him, Brin saw James running down the hallway.

He's going to get himself killed.

Brin did her best to control her facial expressions, to keep her eyes from widening, her face from reacting to seeing James.

He was unarmed. Barefoot and shirtless.

Part of her wanted James to jump on the killer from behind, to wrestle him to the ground. Put him in a chokehold or something. Subdue the killer.

Another part of her knew how ridiculous that was. This wasn't a movie. The man was a cold-blooded killer, one who clearly got off on violence. James—sweet, gentle, nerdy James—didn't stand a chance against him.

Sweet, gentle, nerdy James who also drugged defenseless women into unconsciousness for his own convenience.

Something in her face must have changed at that thought, because the killer's grin suddenly faded. Maybe Brin tipped him off. Maybe he just felt James' presence behind him.

He started to turn to look over his shoulder.

James darted down the side hallway, thankfully.

But the killer was distracted.

Brin's hand brushed against the port bottle.

Now was her chance to save herself.

38

JAMES SEARCHED FRANTICALLY around the office, looking for something he could use as a weapon.

Preferably a projectile weapon.

He'd never liked guns. Never even shot one.

He wished he had one now.

Think, James. What can you use to stop this guy?

He heard the killer speaking in low tones in the kitchen, but couldn't make out what he was saying.

He didn't hear Brin at all.

That was bad.

But, he hadn't heard gunshots or any more crashes.

That was something.

Focus, dammit. Find a weapon.

He had a desk with an iMac and a lamp.

A keyboard.

Brin's cell phone connected to a charging cable.

Tables full of papers and blueprints.

Stacks of books.

James could throw the books. Maybe confuse the killer long enough for Brin to escape.

He could sneak up behind the killer and hit him with the keyboard. Or the lamp. Or even the iMac.

He could smother the killer with the papers, stuff them down his throat and choke him to death.

Goddammit, James.

Focus.

Be realistic.

None of those ideas will work.

He needed a real weapon, something to incapacitate the killer.

He needed to save Brin from this man.

Think, think, think.

James pulled open the cabinets lining the walls. They held office supplies or spare paper or were just empty.

Nothing useful.

He yanked open the drawers to his desk.

Paper clips.

Pens.

A letter opener.

It had a dull rounded tip, but it could be useful in a pinch.

But it wasn't enough. He needed something better.

Maybe a floor lamp from the library would work. The hallway was too narrow to swing it, but he could use it like a lance and ram the killer.

It was a long shot, but James didn't have any better ideas.

Just then, he heard Brin scream.

James was out of time.

Without thinking, acting purely on animal instinct, he lifted the iMac off of his desk, yanking the cables out of their jacks, and ran through the machine room toward the kitchen.

Brin needed him now.

39

Brin's hand closed around the port bottle.

The smooth glass neck was cool in her hand.

The killer was still turning toward the hallway, where James had been a fraction of a second before.

She would only have one shot at this, and she wouldn't have much time.

She had to make this count.

Ignoring the pain in her shoulder and in her leg, Brin forced herself to her feet.

She took one long step toward the killer, landing on the boot of the exoskeleton.

It held her stride firmly. A solid foundation.

She pulled her hand back, the port bottle held firmly by the neck, upside down in her hand.

Against the screams of her shoulder, she swung it forward as hard as she possibly could.

She was going to bash this killer's brains in with a bottle of fucking drug-laced port.

She felt powerful in that moment.

She felt strong.

She felt victorious.

She was about to liberate herself from her own nightmare.

The killer whipped his head back around at her.

With incredible reflexes, his free hand, the hand that wasn't holding the gun, flew up.

It caught the port bottle as Brin brought it crashing down.

The killer caught it flush in his gloved hand.

Brin froze, stunned.

She stared into the hard, dark eyes of the killer, inches from her own.

Her own frightened reflection stared back at her.

The killer wrestled the bottle from Brin with one hard twist of his wrist.

Brin stumbled backward.

The killer examined the bottle.

"What's this, Red?" he said. "You want to get me drunk before we fuck?"

He bit the stopper in his teeth and pulled it free from the bottle, spit it onto the floor.

"Don't mind if I do," he said.

He took a long pull from the bottle.

He stalked toward her, wiping his mouth on the back of his hand.

Brin backed away.

The killer stopped and looked down at the bottle again.

"Damn, that's tasty," he said. He looked up at Brin. "You're a real classy piece, Red."

He took another long pull from the bottle.

"Still gonna kill you, though," he said, that chilling grin coming across his face again.

His teeth were stained red from the wine.

The killer smashed the port bottle down on the floor. Glass shattered everywhere.

The feelings of power, of strength, of victory abandoned Brin in that moment.

In that moment, she felt only panic.

In that moment, with the killer advancing on her, lustful and predatory, she felt only fear.

Brin screamed.

40

IT MAY HAVE BEEN the dumbest possible thing James could have grabbed.

What good was a 27" iMac in a fight?

But in that moment, with his adrenaline pumping, James didn't care.

The computer felt as light to him as a throwing knife.

Which he also carried.

A letter opener, anyway.

It wasn't sharp and it wasn't a gun, but James didn't care about that either.

He only cared about Brin.

She had screamed.

And James had come running.

He wheeled through the machine room and around the corner into the hallway to the kitchen.

What he saw froze his heart.

The killer pointed his gun at Brin.

Brin stumbled backwards down the hallway, toward James.

Something red was splashed everywhere on the floor.

Brin was bleeding.

The killer must have shot her.

But James would have heard the shot.

All of these thoughts flew through James' mind in an instant. But none mattered more than this:

Brin was in danger.

Holding the iMac in front of him like a shield or a massive stone, James ran forward.

He was going to throw the computer at the killer with all the strength he had.

Then he would keep running at him.

Hopefully the computer would hit the killer. Hurt him. At least throw him off balance.

James screamed, a mix of anger and fear and blood rage.

He would kill that man to save Brin.

James knew he would kill to save her.

He watched for the fear to appear in the killer's eyes. Fear from the recognition that nothing would stop James from protecting Brin.

Instead of fear, James saw dead calm in the killer's eyes.

The killer merely aimed his gun toward James.

And fired.

A blaze of fire speared through James' chest.

The force of the bullet knocked him backward.

He'd been charging forward, and the bullet knocked him backward.

He stumbled, then fell on his back. The iMac landed on his chest with a sickening crunch.

James wasn't sure if the crunch was from the computer or his own ribs.

He was numb.

All he could feel was the fire in his chest.

His arms felt numb.

His face felt numb.

He lay on his back under the weight of the computer, staring up at the ceiling. The coffered wood ceiling, painted white.

Brin screamed again.

I'm sorry, Brin.

I'm sorry.

The white coffered ceiling faded to black.

41

Brin ran to James, fell to her knees in front of his body, prone on the floor at the end of the hallway. She shoved the computer off of him.

He was bleeding from a hole in his chest.

"James!" Brin screamed.

She grabbed his bare arms and shook him.

No response.

His chin lifted and his head flopped with the shaking, but James did not stir.

Brin slapped his cheeks.

James just lay limp on the floor, his head rolling from side to side as Brin slapped him.

"How touching," said the killer from behind Brin.

Brin spun on the floor. The killer was walking toward her, his gun pointed at Brin.

"You and your boyfriend are going to die together," he said.

The killer wiped the back of his gloved hand across his eye, squinting and blinking before his eyes refocused on Brin.

"But not before you and me have a little fun," he said.

Brin scrambled backward until she was behind James' body.

"That's it, Red," leered the killer. "Try to run. I like my girls feisty."

Brin wanted to run, wanted to get as far away as she could. But she wouldn't leave James. Not until she was sure he was gone.

And she wasn't willing to admit that to herself just yet.

The killer holstered his gun awkwardly in his pants pocket, catching the barrel on the fabric of the pocket before stuffing the barrel down. He took a staggering side step, then loosened his belt buckle.

He licked his lips slowly, his half-lidded eyes dull as they stared at Brin's half-naked body on the floor in front of him.

Brin could see the man's thoughts in his eyes, in his expression.

They weren't hard to guess.

Her skin crawled.

She hooked her hands under James' armpits and dragged him backward toward the machine room, trying to get his body away from the killer.

She knew it was irrational.

James was probably dead.

Brin should run.

But she wouldn't.

She would make this asshole pay for what he did to James.

Brin dug one bare foot against the gaps in the tile. The other foot, covered in the boot of the exoskeleton, was firm against the ground as she heaved backwards.

James' body was heavy, heavier than Brin had expected. It felt like a giant sack of flour, thick and heavy.

And lifeless.

"Where you going, Red?" said the killer. His voice was slurred slightly.

Still Brin pulled backward. James slid an inch or two, helped by the smooth, cool tile of the hallway floor.

The killer pulled his pants down to his thighs. He wore no underwear, and Brin could see his penis half-erect under the tails of his shirt.

She fought back vomit at the sight.

She lost her grip on James' arms and fell backward into the machine room, sprawled on her back.

As she fell, Brin heard a click.

"Thass how I like 'em," slurred the killer. "Spread on the floor."

The killer shuffled forward, his pants hampering his stride. He tried to step over James, but caught his shoe against James' foot and pitched forward, stumbling until he landed half on James, half on Brin.

His shoulder dug into Brin's stomach, pinning her to the ground. He weighed a ton. Brin could barely move.

Brin could smell the killer's hair. It smelled of oil and musk. She could see his tattoo up close now. Not a dragon at all.

An angel.

Her mind couldn't focus.

That click.

Her mind wanted to be anywhere but here.

Some angel.

Her mind nagged her.

That click.

James suddenly sat up with a great gasp of air. He threw the killer's legs off of him, turned toward Brin.

James' face was ashen. He looked like a dead man.

He was white as an angel.

The killer rolled and squirmed, trying to right himself. He dug his shoulder harder into Brin's stomach.

That click.

James' arm rose high in the air. Something glinted gold in the light.

A knife.

James had a knife in his hand.

His face twisted in anger.

James was alive.

The killer rolled onto his side just as James drove the knife downward. It sank into the killer's torso, on his side near his rib cage.

The killer howled with pain. He grabbed James' head between his hands, squeezed like he could burst James' head with the pressure.

The killer threw James' head against the wall. It made a sickening crunch with the contact.

"James!" screamed Brin.

James slid down the wall until he rested half-seated, half on his side on the floor.

The killer turned to look at the knife sticking out of his side. He pulled it out.

It sounded like someone slurping soup as it came out.

The killer didn't flinch.

That click.

He turned toward Brin, the bloody knife in his hand.

His eyes were dull and unfocused.

When they found Brin, they snapped into focus again.

That click.

The killer's face contorted in rage.

He rolled toward Brin again.

That click!

Brin suddenly remembered what that click meant.

She pulled up her knee just as the killer rolled onto her.

She wedged the boot of the exoskeleton under the killer's body.

Brin had crawled within range of her cell phone.

That click meant the exoskeleton and the phone had reconnected.

Super Brin-style.

The killer reached toward her. Brin flexed her knee, bringing his face closer to hers.

"Yurr deadd," said the killer.

"Sorry, asshole," replied Brin. "Time to fly."

She shoved her leg forward with every ounce of strength she could muster.

The exoskeleton sensed the movement and amplified it.

Just like it had when she'd jumped over the ridge outside.

The killer flew backward with shocking speed.

He slammed against the ceiling.

Brin could hear his bones crack.

The killer's spine broke around the wood coffers like dry spaghetti.

His head cracked against the ceiling, leaving a heavy red stain behind.

He fell to the ground with a wet thump.

Brin rolled over and vomited.

42

Brin stood beside James' hospital bed. Various monitors beeped and flashed and traced thin, wavy lines across their screens. The room, like the entire hospital, reeked of warm bodies, sterile wrappings, and illness.

James was bare-chested and unconscious. Wires ran from round stickers attached at various points across his torso to yet another monitor in the corner.

A tube rose from his mouth with more tubes attached to it. That was breathing for him, the doctors said. James was in an induced coma, they also said, to allow his body to heal. To help the swelling in his brain reduce.

He would eventually recover, they promised, but it would take some time.

Brin wouldn't be there to see it.

She held James' hand. It was limp, but it was warm.

"They say you can hear me, James," she said softly, "so I'll say this." She squeezed his hand, unsure if he could feel it or not.

"Thank you," she said. "Thank you for saving my life."

James had been white as a ghost when Brin had crawled over to him in the hallway. His eyes had been open, but staring blankly at the opposite wall.

Brin had been sure he was dead. She'd wept over him then before forcing herself to call 9-1-1 from her cell phone. She'd had no idea where they were, but the authorities were able to track her signal.

It still took more than an hour for them to get through the forest to James' house. She'd wept over him again until they arrived. When they told her they'd found a pulse, thready and faint, but present, she'd wept again.

The killer, they said, was dead.

That much was obvious from the bloody mess of his body on the floor.

They'd flown James and Brin in the same helicopter to OHSU Hospital in Portland. James went immediately into surgery while they took Brin to a room for examination.

That was the first time Brin had let go of James' hand since they'd loaded him onto his gurney at the house.

Now, it was time for her to let go again.

After a series of x-rays and MRIs, the doctors had shaken their heads, amazed, and told Brin that she was in good health. Her leg was healing nicely and she had no other physical damage.

The police took her then. She had repeated her story at least four times to various officers and detectives before the police had left Brin to the care of the doctors, who insisted she stay overnight for observation, just to be safe.

Now it was morning and Brin was free to go. She'd called her friends, who had been increasingly frantic for days trying to find her. They were on their way to pick her up and take her home at last.

Brin squeezed James' hand again. She thought about the laced port, about James' crazy plan to drug Brin unconscious and drag her out of the forest. She could see that her anger was still there, burning, but distant, like it was trapped in a glass box.

Then she thought about how he'd run madly around the corner carrying a desktop computer to try to fight off her killer. And how he'd risen seemingly from the dead to stab her killer in the side, again trying to save Brin.

And she thought about the care he'd given her, the incredible exoskeleton that had literally saved Brin's life.

It had also left the doctors astounded and excited. They tried to hide it, but they were obviously devastated when Brin refused to let them have James' exoskeleton.

And she thought about the connection she'd had with James. It was real and it was undeniable. She could see that inside her, too, locked in its own glass box.

It had been five wild days in the forest that strained credulity, even for Brin, who had lived through it. If it weren't for the broken leg and James' body laying in the bed before her, Brin would think it had all been a dream.

She couldn't even begin to make sense of it in the cold light of day, standing in a hospital room, back in the real world.

The emotions she felt, both good and bad, were too much for her to process. And far more than she wanted to deal with.

Brin had a life to live.

"Thank you, James," she said again.

She hesitated, but only for a moment, before leaning down to kiss James gently on his forehead. His skin was warm and dry and smelled of a hospital.

It didn't smell like James at all.

She leaned closer, put her mouth beside James' ear.

With her nose beside his long, soft hair, she drew in a deep breath.

That was the smell she would remember.

"I forgive you," she whispered. "Goodbye."

43

THREE WEEKS LATER

James felt like he had been swimming in a grey fog. Sounds drifted through the mist. Beeps and sucking sounds and great banging sounds like a hammer on a steel beam.

And voices. Voices of men and women. Authoritative voices, worried voices, bored voices.

And Brin's voice.

James had clung to Brin's voice.

The sounds all swirled together in that fog, but James reached for Brin's voice in his mind like a drowning man reaching for a rope.

He played it over and over in his mind.

"Thank you," she'd said.

He saw her face. Her bright red hair. Her endless green eyes. They burned bright in his mind.

He knew he was dreaming or delirious. Or dead.

No, probably not dead. Hopefully not dead.

He knew what he saw wasn't real.

But the words were. He felt that to be true.

"Thank you," she'd said.

"Saved my life."

"I forgive you."

James clung to these words like a life raft as he drifted through that grey fog.

Until one night, the fog cleared.

James opened his eyes to a dark room. He could see the dark outline of the television suspended from the ceiling. Through the small rectangular window in the door, he saw a dim light. He wiggled his toes and saw the sheets move at the end of the bed.

James was alive.

James was awake.

Then, he remembered one other thing Brin had said.

"Goodbye."

44

THREE MONTHS LATER

Brin still couldn't believe what she was seeing.

The art gallery was packed with patrons, all sipping white wine and staring at Brin's work on the walls.

And talking about it.

The noise of dozens of conversations echoed off the brick and concrete walls of the trendy gallery near San Francisco's theater district, just a few blocks from the San Francisco Museum of Modern Art.

It was Brin's dream come true. She still had to pinch herself to believe it was really happening.

She started small with a few shows in Portland. She'd met a gallery owner at the coffee shop, talked about art and the business of art while Brin pulled her triple cappuccinos every day for a week until the owner gave Brin her card and offered to take a look at her work, when Brin was ready.

Brin hadn't been ready at all.

But she'd found her creative passion overflowing after her bizarre experience in the Portland forest. Images and artwork flowed from her, first abstract and unfocused, then increasingly detailed and specific. Brin was re-creating that experience, pouring all of her intense and conflicting emotions into art.

No one would know it, really, unless Brin explained it to them. They would have had to experience it themselves to understand.

But the art was alive, more than anything Brin had created before. The gallery owner responded immediately and booked first one show, then another, then several more. Brin's art drew more and more attention. Her fourth show sold out.

She moved into a bigger space for three more shows and sold those out, too.

That's when a patron approached her with an offer for a show in San Francisco. She would need dozens of new pieces to fill the space, but it was Brin's big break. An art show in a prestigious gallery in San Francisco was Brin's ticket to stardom in the art world.

At least, it was to her.

And now she was here.

She stood half hidden in the shadow of a hallway leading to the back of the gallery, observing the patrons. She was dressed in a slim, elegant evening gown with two-inch heels. She'd never dressed so fancy in her life, but wanted to look the part for her patrons. She would have to make an entrance later to meet them.

The patrons gazed at her work, some on large canvases that covered entire walls, others small enough to set on a kitchen counter. Some were fiery, others cool. Some expressed fear, others anger, others amazement.

And some expressed pure, unadulterated love.

The patrons discussed possible meanings. They talked about Brin's use of color or line, about the energy of her paint strokes and her compositional choices.

But Brin saw her soul, her heart laid bare.

She was telling her story in the most complete and accurate way she knew how.

But there was only one person in the world who could possibly hear it.

"Funny," said a voice behind where Brin stood. "That's not quite how I remember it."

Brin's heart leapt into her throat. A smile broke upon her face before she could control it.

She composed herself before turning.

James wore a slim navy suit coat over a deep blue button-down shirt tucked into dark jeans, and elegant boots. He'd cut his hair back to just over his ears and was sporting a tidy beard.

He looked gorgeous.

With one hand in his pocket, he cradled a glass of wine in the other as he looked across the room at a massive painting on the opposite wall.

"I thought you don't drink wine," said Brin as she moved to stand beside James, her heels clicking against the smooth concrete floor.

James shrugged without looking at her.

"Helps to blend in with the natives," he said. "Don't want to attract attention, you know."

"That a problem for you?" Brin asked. "Attracting attention?"

"Used to be," said James. "Not anymore."

He set the full glass on the tray of a server walking by, then clasped his hands in front of him.

"You see," he said, "I remember that night—and morning, of course—as more blue, really. Not so orange."

"Is that right?" Brin replied.

"Not a cold blue, mind you," James said. "Definitely not that. But a soft blue. A warm blue."

"Blue is a cool color, you know," Brin said.

"That's what made it so incredible, you see?"

James turned to Brin. He fixed those clear brown eyes onto

hers and the rest of the room faded to the background until Brin and James were the only two people in the entire world.

"That blue was the warmest, most soothing, most comfortable color I've ever seen," James continued. "It felt absolutely, perfectly right. That's what was so incredible."

Brin stepped a half-step closer to James.

He stepped toward her.

They were close enough that Brin could smell James' scent, like sunshine and warm leather.

"Is that the only thing that was incredible?" asked Brin, her voice low and husky.

A strand of her hair fell across her face. James reached out and smoothed it back into place.

The touch of his hand sent shock waves through Brin's body.

"No," whispered James. "Not even close."

ACKNOWLEDGMENTS

Undying thanks to Kim and Gail for their help in editing this novel. The collective groans of a thousand readers have been averted by your keen eyes.

As always, my love and thanks to Holly. Without your support, my love, none of this would be possible.

MORE FROM THE AUTHOR

To learn more about Kevin Robert Aldrich and stay up-to-date with all of his stories and novels, please visit his website:

www.kevinrobertaldrich.com.

To be automatically notified with every new release, join the Kevin Robert Aldrich mailing list!

Join the list!